"Are you [...]

Cameron look [...]
to go back?"

Gabrielle didn't know what to say. His question had thrown her off. "Whether you go back or not isn't up to me."

"Well, no, I'm not interested in going back. Now, if you were to ask me in, I'd accept the invite before you released your next breath."

Unsure of herself and Cameron, Gabrielle wished she could give him an answer. Telling him to go home was rude—and she wasn't sure that was what she really wanted.

Cameron didn't give her much time to think. His urge to taste her mouth had won out over his attempt to cool himself down. Lifting her chin with two fingers, Cameron lowered his head until their lips met. To gauge her reaction, he dusted her lips with several soft kisses. Then his forefinger slowly outlined her mouth.

Looking into her mesmerizing eyes, Cameron tried to see if he'd moved too fast or had been inappropriate. She appeared a bit startled but didn't seem to object to his show of affection. The blush on her cheeks was a telltale sign.

Giving it no more thought, he let his top lip skirt her bottom one, causing her breath to come in short spurts. She hadn't pushed him away. He took it as a good sign and hoped he wasn't making a mistake. He didn't want to lose her, and he already cared enough for her to risk his heart again.

Books by Linda Hudson-Smith

Kimani Romance

Forsaking All Others
Indiscriminate Attraction
Romancing the Runway
Destiny Calls
Kissed by a Carrington
Promises to Keep
Seduction at Whispering Lakes
Tempted by a Carrington
Waves of Passion

LINDA HUDSON-SMITH

was born in Canonsburg, Pennsylvania, and raised in Washington, Pennsylvania. After illness forced her to leave a successful marketing and public relations career, she turned to writing as a healing and creative outlet.

Linda has won several awards, including a Career Achievement Award from *RT Book Reviews*. She was voted Best New Writer by the Black Writers Alliance, named Best New Christian Fiction Author by *Shades of Romance* magazine and Rising Star by *Romance in Color*. She is also a recipient of a Gold Pen award and has won two awards from The African American Literary Awards Show.

For the past decade Linda has served as a national spokesperson for the Lupus Foundation of America.

The mother of two sons, Linda lives with her husband, Rudy, in League City, Texas. To find out more, go to her website, www.lindahudsonsmith.com. You can also email her at lindahudsonsmith@yahoo.com.

Waves
of
PASSION

LINDA HUDSON-SMITH

HARLEQUIN®
entertain, enrich, inspire™

ISBN-13: 978-0-373-86271-9

WAVES OF PASSION

Dear Reader,

I sincerely hope you enjoy reading *Waves of Passion* from cover to cover. It features doctors Gabrielle Grinage and Cameron Quinn, who are on duty aboard a cruise ship as they sail from one exotic port to another in the Caribbean.

I'm very interested in hearing your comments on the romance between Dr. Quinn and Dr. Grinage.

Please send a stamped self-addressed envelope to Linda Hudson-Smith, 16516 El Camino Real, Box 174, Houston, TX 77062.

www.lindahudsonsmith.com

lindahudsonsmith@yahoo.com

Chapter 1

It was early April, the day before Dr. Gabrielle Grinage's official duties were to begin on a new job. She was unable to control her quivering stomach, yet her hazel eyes drank in the unfamiliar surroundings as slender fingers smoothed her thick, chestnut-brown French braid.

Here I am. Only the passage of time will let me know if my choice was a wise one.

Comfortably seated in the front row of a new employee orientation seminar/luncheon, Gabrielle felt at peace aboard the extravagantly beautiful cruise ship, the *Parisian Paradise*. This magnificent cruise liner was one of many fabulous ships that sailed under the popular Fantasy Islands Fleet. As she listened intently to the speaker, her eyes encompassed him.

"Ah, here he is," Grey Sadler enthusiastically announced, "Dr. Cameron Quinn. This is the enormously talented medical commander you'll take orders from. I have to warn you, Dr. Quinn is a tyrant and he expects nothing less than excellence and dedication from his medical staff." Grey chuckled. "He's also a phenomenal doctor and one of the fairest people I know."

As Dr. Quinn strolled to the podium, he held his head high and his shoulders back. After shaking the hand of the cruise director, he positioned himself at the podium. Cameron's smoky black eyes roved the vast group of new and veteran employees. His porcelain white teeth and gleaming smile captured the audience's attention and his deep voice raptly held it.

"Welcome to each of you! It's a privilege and an honor to have you on my staff." Cameron's eyes shone brightly. "All I expect from you is your absolute very best. I require my staff to attend every training session and to be present at all personnel meetings. We have to be a tightly knit group on this ship, and I demand that we work as a close unit."

Dr. Quinn spoke about the rigid policies and specific rules that governed the ship's infirmary and its personnel. He gave a brief summary of his educational background and his amazing career history. His extensive travels to numerous exotic locations around the world were touched upon fleetingly. He casually mentioned that he was thirty-three. His single status produced broad smiles from different groups of females seated close by.

"I want each new staff member to feel like they're a part of our medical family. If not, we'll figure out why they don't. Our team relies on and believes in each other. We're together for hours on end, so we must learn how to cohabitate harmoniously. Welcome aboard the magnificent *Parisian Paradise!*" He raised his water glass in a toast.

Gabrielle couldn't take her eyes off Cameron. She guessed his height to be around six-two or six-three. His physique boasted a tapered waistline and remarkably broad chest and shoulders. She imagined him sporting a six-pack wall of impenetrable steel abs beneath his stark-white shirt. Sewn onto each shoulder of the shirt were gold symbols indicating his official ranking and gold braided medical insignias. Around his neck he wore an anchor on a thick gold chain.

Cameron Quinn, M.D., was gorgeous and, from all indications, highly intelligent. Curly and satiny, his dark brown hair had premature graying at the temples. His clean-shaven, olive-brown complexion only added to his good looks. His fit physique was perfectly proportioned with his stature. From Gabrielle's standpoint, he had it going on in looks, but she was more curious as to what his intellect would bring to the table.

Cameron took a gulp of water. "Our crew always has each other's backs, and we never indulge in petty arguing and backbiting. As staff members, we may not agree on every issue, but we'll eventually work things out. Again, welcome aboard the magnificent *Parisian Paradise!*"

A standing ovation took place as Dr. Quinn left the podium.

Cameron Quinn had impressed Gabrielle greatly. His personality was refreshing.

If he's as easy to work with as he is to look at and listen to, we should get along just fine.

Practicing medicine on a cruise ship hadn't been one of Gabrielle's goals during medical school, and she'd only recently opted to give it a try. The chance to travel to exotic ports had also figured into her decision. Several of her friends in the medical field worked aboard cruise ships…and they positively loved it. The salary was decent and the living arrangements would save her from financially draining monthly expenses. Five months onboard with five weeks off was a normal work schedule for doctors, nurses and various other medical staffers.

Gabrielle didn't think that two or three years away from a private career in an internal practice would hurt her chances of getting back into mainstream medicine. She was only thirty and had lots of good years ahead of her. Deep thoughts, along with playing the devil's advocate, had helped to guide her to this decision. Treating those in need of excellent health care was in her DNA.

Born and raised in Galveston, Texas, the ship's homeport, she felt privileged to sail each seven-day itinerary from her birthplace. The *Parisian Paradise* docked for several hours. And Gabrielle planned to meet her family when time permitted.

Gabrielle knew what she'd like to do with her leisure time—get to know Cameron.

Gabrielle watched Cameron's every move. He walked with confidence, holding his head up as if he knew he was a man to be reckoned with. As he took time to shake hands and speak with other attendees, she studied him closely, pleasantly surprised that he hadn't headed straight for the table occupied by all the powers that be. Growing more and more curious about the man she was to work directly under, she could hardly wait for their first encounter.

Gabrielle took notice of everything that happened close to where she sat. She got a good feeling about the crew. She was optimistic and hoped she'd fit in well.

When the meeting adjourned, the dark-haired woman who was seated next to Gabrielle turned to her. She held out a friendly hand in greeting. "I'm Marjorie Carson, a crewmember and an R.N. Welcome aboard! It's probably a safe bet that we'll work together. Do you want to get something to eat and drink?"

Gabrielle briefly took Marjorie's hand. "Thank you. I'm Gabrielle Grinage, M.D. I'm sure we'll share many shifts, and I'd love for us to break bread together. I noticed that they were laying out covered dishes and bread baskets as orientation wound down. It smells divine."

Marjorie nodded in agreement. "They lay it out big during employee events. Like Dr. Quinn said, we're one big happy family

"I take it that you're not a new employee. How long have you worked on the *Parisian Paradise?*"

"I've been assigned to this ship for two years," Marjorie responded. "And I love it. I joined the luxury cruise line profession at twenty-six. I'm now twenty-eight."

Gabrielle nodded, smiling. "Are you contracted for five months on and five weeks off?"

"One and the same, Dr. Grinage. I like the schedule. Looks like we'd better claim a table then get in line before it gets too crowded," Marjorie said.

"Good suggestion." Gabrielle smiled as she got to her feet.

The two women quickly claimed a premier window booth. Once the waiter poured ice water and iced tea into crystal goblets, the ladies headed toward the buffet lines. Marjorie chatted up Gabrielle about some of the infirmary duties.

Back at the table within minutes, carrying plates loaded with salads and seafood, the two women wasted no time in dipping into their food.

"Tell me a little about yourself, that is, if you don't mind," Marjorie suggested.

Gabrielle gave a brief rundown on her educational background before getting into personal areas. "I'm happily single." She held up her bare ring finger. "My parents and three of my four brothers practice medicine. Mom and Dad are retired internal medicine specialists."

As the only female sibling, Gabrielle told Marjorie, her family had nearly spoiled her rotten. No one in the Grinage clan had vocally approved or disapproved of where and how she'd chosen to practice medicine. Her decision to treat patients on a cruise ship had come as a total shock to them. However, everyone in the family was encouraged to choose their own destiny.

Marjorie appeared very interested in what Gabrielle shared. "What do your brothers do in the wide-open field of medicine?"

Gabrielle laid a napkin across her lap. "Ryan, the oldest, is an anesthesiologist, and Maxwell is an OB/GYN. Jonathan, the next to the youngest, is a pediatrician. Christopher is a hospital administrator…and a Ph.D."

Gabrielle's brothers, Ryan and Maxwell, were partners in a very successful private practice. None of the siblings were married and they all lived locally. Both parents had contributed thirty-five years of work in the medical field to Galveston Island residents.

"Wow! An entire family working in the medical field is awesome," Marjorie said.

"It is amazing." Gabrielle glanced around the room, hoping to get another glimpse of Cameron. Much to her surprise, many of the attendees had formed a line to meet him. He was seated alone at a large table. "Is meeting Dr. Quinn part of the orientation?"

Marjorie shook her head. "Not formally, but most people want to meet him. Like me, everyone here isn't a new employee. Many of us return to this orientation just to mingle and greet the ship's newcomers. Dr. Quinn has attended every orientation since I've been here. Do you want to meet him?"

Gabrielle chuckled. "Not if I have to stand in a long line." She grew silent, looking toward the end of the line. "It'll take an hour or more to get to him. Maybe I'll go over when the crowd thins."

"You won't be sorry. He's approachable and very easy to talk to. He's popular with the entire crew."

Gabrielle's eyes strayed back to Dr. Quinn—and she really liked what she saw.

Marjorie laughed. "You're taking a real good look at the single and available Dr. Quinn. The man is so down-to-earth. I don't know a single soul who doesn't like working with him."

Gabrielle turned her attention back to Marjorie. "That's good to know. Arrogant pretty boys don't interest me, but I'd love to have a great working relationship with Dr. Quinn. Maybe you can stop by his table with me once we finish eating."

Marjorie smiled. "I'd be happy to introduce you two."

A good-looking male suddenly called out to Marjorie from a short distance away.

A huge smile brightened Marjorie's mocha complexion. "That's Tristan Meadows heading this way. He's also a nurse…and he has a crush on me," Marjorie whispered lowly, looking around for her napkin.

Watching the rapidly approaching Tristan, Gabrielle lifted an eyebrow. He was nearly as handsome as the commander. His body wasn't as chiseled as Cameron's, yet he had a solid physique. His broad smile revealed shining white teeth.

"Hey, ladies," Tristan said cheerfully. He extended his tawny-brown hand to Gabrielle and added, "Welcome aboard the *Parisian Paradise*. I'm Tristan Meadows. It's a pleasure meeting you."

Gabrielle shook his hand. "Nice to meet you, too, Tristan. I'm Gabrielle Grinage."

Tristan sat down next to Marjorie. "So you're the new doctor? I look forward to working with you, Dr. Grinage," he said with sincerity.

Gabrielle smiled. "I'd be happy if you both called me by my first name. No titles are necessary." Hoping to put him at ease, Gabrielle gave him a warm smile.

Tristan smiled back at Gabrielle. "You can count on it." His dark brown eyes softened as he gazed into Marjorie's ebony eyes. "Perhaps you can put in a good word for me with Marjorie. She's not taking me seriously."

"Tristan, stop it," Marjorie weakly demanded, her mocha cheeks flushed with embarrassment. "Gabrielle is not interested in our personal lives. Put a lid on it."

Gabrielle's laughter trilled. "I'm interested in the lives of anyone I'm privileged to work with. But, Tristan, I can't possibly put in a good word for you. That is, not until I get to know if you'd be good for Marjorie."

Everyone laughed.

Gabrielle looked across the room and saw that the

lines leading to Dr. Quinn had thinned considerably. Feeling courageous, she stood. "I'll be back. It's time to meet my boss."

"Decided to go it alone, huh? Good for you," Marjorie said.

After telling the couple to save her seat, Gabrielle excused herself.

The butterflies suddenly occupying her stomach had Gabrielle's insides quivering again. With only a few people ahead of her, she felt sweat forming on her palms. She had no clue why she was so nervous, but she couldn't rule out the fabulous looks and the suave demeanor of the commander, the man she would soon work closely with.

Cameron got to his feet just as Gabrielle reached him. He instantly extended his hand to her. "Hello, Dr. Grinage. I'm glad we're finally meeting. Please allow me to personally welcome you aboard your new home."

"Thank you, Dr. Quinn." Overwhelmed by his warm attention, Gabrielle had a hard time finding her voice. "It's nice to meet the commander I've heard so much about."

"Please sit down," Cameron offered. "I'd like to hear what you've heard."

Before taking a seat, she looked behind her, surprised to see she was last in line. She took in a few calming breaths as she sat. "What I've heard has been good. I also read your medical bio inside the orientation packet. It was amazing." The absence of a picture had made her wonder what he might look like.

Cameron grinned. "I've also read your bio. I was impressed. You come from quite a medical family. My parents own and manage a couple of apartment buildings in Houston. They're very happy with their lives, but they wanted their only son to be a doctor."

Gabrielle frowned. "You became a doctor for your family?"

Cameron laughed. "If it hadn't also been my own dream, I couldn't have accomplished it. My mom always talks about how I loved to play doctor when I was little. I love being a physician. More than that, I love helping those in need."

"I know what you mean. Helping others is one of the main reasons I wanted to be a physician. I also played doctor. My little male chauvinist friends thought I should be the nurse, but I had bigger and brighter ideas."

Cameron laughed. "Sounds like you took charge. What made you want to try practicing medicine on the high seas?"

Gabrielle looked thoughtful. "I'm adventurous by nature. I like to try new things. I heard most of the pros and cons from friends who work on cruise ships. I took everything I learned into consideration, then I decided to just try it."

Cameron smiled. "I think you'll find the job rewarding and enjoyable, just as I do. Working on a cruise ship is altogether different from the world of medicine we started out in. We're more limited here, and if it comes to drastic measures, we often have to make arrangements for emergency transportation to take patients to a hospital on land."

Gabrielle nodded. "I researched it a lot before I actually signed on. I'm eager to learn the ways of practicing medicine at sea."

Cameron smiled. "I bet you're a fast learner." He looked up and saw that other greeters had arrived. He instantly got to his feet. "Excuse me for a few minutes. A line has formed again."

Gabrielle stood, her heart beating faster than normal. "You go right ahead. I'll see you again." For sure, she'd see him in the infirmary tomorrow morning.

Before Cameron could protest her departure, Gabrielle had already stepped away.

The line had dissipated after twenty minutes or so, and Cameron reclaimed his seat at the table. As his eyes searched the room for Gabrielle, he couldn't help thinking of how enjoyable her company had been. Working with her would be a great experience, as long as he was careful not to compromise his heart. She was alluring, a natural beauty, but he knew she had a lot more going for her than that. The excellent academic and work ethics written up in her bio had revealed that.

His mind turned to thoughts of the scores of single women who came aboard the ship and sailed away into the sunset. Once the cruise was over, they left the ship without looking back. He knew that getting involved with female passengers wasn't an ideal situation for him.

Gabrielle was the first female doctor he'd worked with aboard a ship, but he still had to remain in tight control of himself. Mixing business with pleasure could be a devastating combination. Cameron also had firsthand knowledge of that.

Finding true love was hard to do, especially on a cruise.

Gabrielle noticed that her heart was still beating fast even after a quick break in the ladies' room. She made her way back to the table, where Marjorie and Tristan didn't look as if they'd missed her presence. She stood quietly and watched the hot chemistry at work. They made a great couple.

As Gabrielle sat down, she cleared her throat. "I'm back."

Marjorie appeared slightly embarrassed. "What did you think of Dr. Quinn?"

Gabrielle smiled. "I can't tell you that until after I spend more time in his company. But he seems kind and smart. I'm willing to bet he's also sweet. But since we'll be working together, there is no chance for a ship-board romance. Love and labor don't mix."

Tristan raised an eyebrow. "I beg to differ. Love and labor go hand in hand. If you can find something special with someone you work with, go for it. Being employed in the same profession is a pretty good start, anyway. At least you'll have something in common."

"I agree," Marjorie chimed in. "It's nice to have someone to talk to about your work."

Tristan covered Marjorie's hand with his. "If you feel that way, then why can't I get you to take me seriously?"

Marjorie now looked totally embarrassed. "I do."

"You do what?" Tristan asked, putting her on the spot.

Marjorie blushed. "I take you seriously. I really do."

Tristan's broad smile showed he was pleased as punch. "I'm glad to hear it. But why'd you suddenly change your mind? I've been chasing you for months."

Marjorie's eyes narrowed. "I wasn't ready to be caught. Can we just leave it at that?"

Gabrielle wanted to laugh at these two dopey lovebirds, but she remained quiet, eager to hear what else they had to say.

"I'm happy to leave it at that if it means I can take you out on a real date," Tristan said.

Marjorie smiled. "You can take me out, Tristan. I'd love to see tonight's show."

Tristan leaned over and kissed Marjorie's cheek. "It's a date."

Gabrielle laughed. "Congratulations on your first real date!"

The living quarters assigned to Gabrielle were located a few decks above midship. The spacious suite wasn't particularly lavish, but it was nice and homey and it had a balcony. She'd never lived in a place with such a wide-open concept, where she could see the living room, kitchen and bedroom all at once. Only the bathroom was in a separate room.

As Gabrielle closely studied the space, she felt its warmth. Her personal things had already been delivered, but she hadn't had time to put them away. She hadn't even paid a lot of attention to the suite's floor plan until now. Luckily the balcony would offer her a nearby outdoor alternative. Being able to step outside and breathe in fresh air without having to go up on deck was a huge plus. The balcony was decked out with a small round table, two chairs and a chaise lounge to lie on to catch the sun. This suite was her home for the next five months, so she would have to get used to it.

The *Parisian Paradise* was a huge vessel, which gave Gabrielle plenty of indoor and outdoor spaces to explore and many choices in shopping, dining and entertainment venues. She also loved that room service was available to staff and passengers 24/7.

Gabrielle caught sight of her unpacked luggage and frowned. For her to be truly comfortable, she had to put everything in order right away. There was plenty of time for her to unpack and get it over with before reporting to duty in the morning. After taking off her uniform and hanging it up, she slipped into blue jeans and a white T-shirt.

Starting with a leather garment bag, she took out her dressier and formal attire and hung them at one end of the large sectional closet. She then moved on to the suitcases.

A couple of hours later, she had the cabin suite looking more like a home.

Deciding to do a little bit of exploring, Gabrielle pulled from the closet a pair of white pants and a gold silk top. As she pulled on the attire, her eyes searched the room for her makeup case. The moment she spotted it next to the leather sofa, she felt totally relieved that she hadn't left it behind. Standing before the bathroom mirror, Gabrielle was pleased with her appearance. She loved how her long hair fell around her shoulders and how flawlessly she had applied her makeup. Gabrielle picked up her gold purse and dropped her cabin key inside. Just as she stepped out the door, Cameron came out of the cabin right next to hers. He looked sexy dressed in dark dress slacks and a powder-blue silk shirt. She couldn't help wondering if his assigned quarters were really that close to hers or if he'd been visiting someone.

As Cameron's eyes fell upon her, she felt butterflies

in her stomach. His devastating smile made her weak in the knees. "Seeing you so soon is a nice surprise."

Cameron walked the few steps to where she stood. "I was hoping to see you before we began working together. Have you made any special plans?"

Gabrielle shrugged with nonchalance. "I just decided to do a little exploring."

He grinned. "Perhaps I could be your tour guide for the evening. Would you mind?"

"Not at all." Gabrielle was pleased by his offer. "It'd be easy to get lost on this vessel."

"It happens often, Dr. Grinage. One wrong turn can get you all out of sorts. How about starting on the fifth level where most of the live action is?"

Gabrielle smiled brightly. "It's fine with me. Lead the way, Dr. Quinn."

He stopped short of offering her his arm. It was inappropriate. "I'd like it if you'd simply call me Cameron. Is it okay to call you Gabrielle? It's a lovely name."

"Thank you, Cameron. I like being on a first-name basis with my coworkers."

The neon lights and glamorous decor found on Parisian Boulevard astounded Gabrielle. She'd never taken a cruise before, and she was amazed. A bevy of specialty shops shone inside and out with dazzling lights. The colorful and brightly lit Champs-Elysées Casino was located on the same level. Cameron gave her a brief tour of the gambling facility. It wasn't his favorite place to hang out because he didn't like throwing away hard-earned money.

"All these bells and lights from the slot machines and screams from winners are exciting," Gabrielle said.

He shrugged. "True enough, but there's a downside to the excitement. The cruise liners make it easy for people to gamble away their money by borrowing funds against their credit card. Most people think they can make up the losses."

Gabrielle hunched her shoulders. "I've never gambled. I'm not sure I can feed money into an inanimate object and expect it to pay me back handsomely. But from the excited sounds in here, there seems to be lots of winners."

"Most definitely, but far more are losers," Cameron remarked. "It's one thing to have fun gambling and something totally different to be addicted."

"I hadn't thought of that. But I don't have to worry about it. I'm a cheapskate, a budgeter. I don't just give away money."

"I wish I knew how to keep a tighter budget. I tend to splurge every now and then, but I usually have something to show for it. Maybe you can give me some pointers."

"You got it. I have a great book on financial planning in my cabin. You can read it if you'd like. It helped me out a lot."

"If you don't mind bringing it to the clinic tomorrow, I'll take good care of it."

Gabrielle nodded. "You'll have it in the morning."

As the tour proceeded, Cameron showed Gabrielle both formal dining rooms, the Paris and the Marseille.

"Let's go back to Parisian Boulevard," Cameron suggested. "There's plenty of duty-free shops."

As Cameron and Gabrielle made their way back to Parisian Boulevard, they passed by several music venues. It seemed to her that music was offered all over the ship, like the live calypso and reggae she'd heard inside and outside on the main deck for hours on end. There was even a jumbo LED screen that showed special movies, concerts, sports and other entertainment.

"Would you like to get something to drink?" Cameron asked.

"All this walking has me a bit thirsty. I'd like a cold soda or iced tea." Gabrielle was glad she'd chosen to wear flat sandals. In heels, her feet would have taken a good pounding.

"We'll go into one of the lounges where we can listen to music. I don't hang out on the ship very often. Even though the clinic closes at 6:00 p.m., one doctor is always on call. As the medical commander, I'm the backup and go-to person if two doctors are needed."

"I know that there's minimal free time. Still, I'm pleased with my decision."

Cameron chuckled. "Let's see how you feel after the first month."

Gabrielle eyed him with curiosity. "Is that a warning?"

"Hardly. I just want to know your thoughts after working aboard for a while."

"I'll be sure to tell you. Have any of your crew members been unhappy?"

"That's an understatement. There are some folks who can't hack it. They think the job is glamour and glitz until they're aboard for a week or so. Most of those who quit leave very early. It doesn't take long for the boys and girls to separate themselves from the men and women."

Gabrielle smiled. "If I didn't know better, I'd think you were trying to scare me."

Cameron stopped and looked into Gabrielle's eyes. "I'm just answering. I'd never frighten you on purpose."

Feeling herself getting lost in his intense gaze, Gabrielle looked away. "I won't ask any more questions. I'll wait and see what happens with me."

The urge to take her hand to reassure her pulled at Cameron, but he didn't dare. Holding her hand was too intimate for what could only be a working relationship between them. Although he found her extremely attractive and very sexy, he had to abide by his own rules, no matter how hard it might become.

At the Cannes Lounge Gabrielle and Cameron were escorted to a table near the piano bar by a hostess with a bubbly personality. Once they were seated, she took their drink orders and left.

Cameron settled back in the plush chair. "This is a nice place to relax. The guy who plays the piano and sings is excellent. He normally does the top forty and on some nights he plays oldies but goodies. Do you like the karaoke scene?"

Gabrielle chuckled. "I love to listen to people who can't sing, yet are brave enough to get up there and give it a shot. I don't have that kind of courage. What about you?"

"I don't sound too bad, but I'd have to be feeling pretty good to put myself on display. I do sing in the shower though."

"I—" Gabrielle cut her response short as the hostess set the drinks on the table.

"What were you going to say?" Cameron asked.

"I also sing in the shower. The sound of my own voice isn't that bad to me, though it might be terrifying to others." She chuckled then lifted her glass of iced tea. "Here's to us building a great working relationship, Cameron. I believe we'll work well together."

Cameron raised his glass. "Hear, hear. We've already managed to break the ice quite nicely. If there is anything you need help with on the job, don't be afraid to let me know. I'm a great supervisor, Gabrielle, a really fair and patient one."

Gabrielle smiled softly. "I can believe that about you. You seem down-to-earth."

The couple smiled warmly at each other as they clinked together their glasses.

Freshly showered and ready for bed, Gabrielle climbed in between the sheets. She had a feeling that she wouldn't be sleeping alone tonight. Cameron's strong presence wasn't going away anytime soon. The great impression he'd made on her would stay with her for a long time. She wouldn't mind him sleeping next to her, even if it was only in her dreams. Sighing, Gabrielle positioned the extra pillow against her abdomen and wrapped her arms around it.

Chapter 2

Seated on the chaise lounge, Gabrielle waited for the sun to make its appearance. In the city she'd never seen this many bright stars in the sky at night, unless she was near a beach in her hometown. It was a breathtaking experience. Awed by the vision, she sighed. The sea was calm and she finally felt the same. The slight movement of the ship was hypnotic. Although the humongous vessel cut through the waters with great speed, she could barely feel it.

It was still very early in the morning, but Gabrielle had slept fitfully throughout the night. She had tossed and turned repeatedly, as had her mind. The last time she'd awakened, she hadn't been able to get back to sleep. With dawn so close, she'd gotten out of bed to experience a sunrise at sea. She'd put on a white velour bathrobe, then stepped out onto the balcony and been instantly welcomed with a warm breeze.

From the moment Gabrielle's head had hit the pillow, just before midnight, her thoughts had been filled with the fantastic time she'd spent with Cameron. He was a true gentleman, and she already liked him a lot. His shaking her hand before they'd departed had spoken volumes. It saddened her that they couldn't have a romantic liaison, but she'd find contentment in working alongside him in the clinic. He wasn't the first desirable man to be off-limits to her.

Gabrielle reminded herself that she was here to do a job, which she felt was an amazing experience, one that she'd never have on land. She was eager to learn as much as she could from Cameron. By the time her first five months were up, she'd be able to execute the most important procedures and policies of the clinic.

There had been so many personal questions she had wanted to ask Cameron but she hadn't dared to. Whether he had a current girlfriend or fiancée was constantly on her mind. She couldn't imagine a man as good-looking as him without a woman, but she also figured it might be hard for him to get involved with anyone aboard the ship, especially anyone from his staff.

There wasn't a shortage of females on the cruise, but he hadn't seemed to notice anyone in particular last night. He'd given her his undivided attention. She had delighted in every moment of it despite the fact that they would never be anything other than coworkers.

Getting up from the chaise lounge, she leaned over the railing and stared down onto the dark waters. To help clear her head, she inhaled deeply. The air didn't smell polluted. In fact, there wasn't any kind of unpleasant scent wafting upward from the sea.

The perfectly formed sun appeared to rise majestically right out of the ocean. Slowly, unambiguously, the round, orangey-yellow ball of dazzling light wended its way into the heavens. With a smile on her face, she watched the incredible ascent.

Freshly showered, with only a bath towel wrapped around his waist, Cameron stood in front of the bathroom mirror in his cabin suite. As he carefully shaved overnight stubble, he couldn't keep his mind off Gabrielle. He could still smell the beguiling perfume that had tantalized and teased his nostrils unmercifully all evening. Nuzzling her neck with his nose had been a constant temptation for him, making him wish things could be different.

An image of her long chestnut hair flowing like a silk curtain had stayed with him. He'd wondered if she wore the thick single French braid only when working. The hairstyle was flattering, but it hardly rivaled the sex appeal of its full-bodied silkiness sweeping her shoulders. As they'd strolled around the open deck, taking in the sights and sounds, the stirring winds had played in her hair, making his fingers itch for the same privilege.

Once Cameron finished shaving and brushing his teeth, he splashed on his favorite aftershave and cologne. Finished with his toiletries, he hastily left the bathroom and went into the bedroom, where he slipped on his white uniform.

Cameron sat on the side of the bed as he put a call in to room service, his regular morning ritual. He cheerfully greeted the person on the other line then made his usual order: one egg over medium, sausages, hot oatmeal, a carton of milk and hot coffee.

* * *

Surprised by the knock on her door so early, Gabrielle asked who was there as she peered out the security window.

"Room service," replied a male voice.

After removing the safety locks, Gabrielle opened the door. Frowning slightly, she looked at the tray the young man held. "There must be a mistake. I didn't order room service."

The man peered at the order slip. "This is the cabin number on the order. Can I please come in and set down the tray?"

Shrugging her shoulders, Gabrielle moved aside. She knew this was a mistake, no matter what the delivery person said. He didn't seem in the mood to argue the point and neither was she. The delicious aroma of hot coffee had already tempted her palate. Once he'd laid the food items out on the table, he nodded and left the suite.

Gabrielle walked over to the door and reengaged the safety locks. Eager for a sip of coffee, she made a quick jaunt to the table and fixed it to her liking. Savoring the hot brew, she closed her eyes. As she reopened them, she looked over the array of food.

It appeared somebody else liked many of the same things she did. An egg over medium was her favorite, and she loved hot oatmeal with milk and sugar. She could take or leave the sausage links, but she wouldn't waste them. Toast with strawberry preserves was the breakfast she ate most mornings, but there wasn't any in the order.

A slip of paper with handwriting on it suddenly caught her eye. She picked it up and read it. "Good morning, Gabrielle. I hope you enjoy your first break-fast aboard the *Parisian Paradise*. I hope I ordered some of your favorites. Since these happen to be a few of mine, I thought I'd order you the same. See you later on in the clinic. My very best, Cameron."

A pleasantly surprised look glowed on her face. "Oh, my goodness, what made Cameron do this? How sweet." They hadn't discussed their food likes and dis-likes, but he'd gotten so many of hers right. She racked her brain, wondering if any of the employment question-naires she'd filled out had asked about her food choices.

It's silly of me to keep questioning this. Cameron's note spelled it all out.

Careful not to take his kind gesture out of context, Gabrielle decided to wait until she got to the clinic to thank him instead of calling him. She still didn't know if that was his cabin he'd come out of last evening. She'd been self-conscious about what he'd think of the ques-tion, so she hadn't brought it up.

A glance at the clock let Gabrielle know she still had a little over two hours before she had to report for duty. Picking up the fork, she took her first bite of egg, wish-ing she had toast to dip into the yolk. She was hungrier than she'd thought, and she polished off her meal in a matter of minutes.

Ready for a second cup of coffee, Gabrielle went over to the coffeemaker and brewed a single serving. While waiting for it, she walked over to the bookshelf and pulled down one of the numerous photo albums she'd brought from home. Missing her family had sud-denly prompted the idea of looking at family photos.

The very first photo inside the album was of the en-tire family taken during the Christmas holidays. Her mother and father's unconditional love for her seemed to leap from the pages and wrap around her like a warm blanket. She wouldn't trade Emma and Ross Grinage for all the money in the world. They had never been too busy for their children. With her being the only girl, they'd made sure she had her fair share of special attention. She was the apple of her father's eye and always doted on by her mother.

Looking at the picture of her handsome brothers made Gabrielle smile. These guys had taken care of her as though she was their very own child. She had wanted for nothing as she'd grown up. Her brothers had even taken turns combing and brushing her hair. When she'd begun dating, her boyfriends had gotten trouble from her brothers. She had always felt cherished and protected by them—and up to this day they still looked out for her.

The next few pages of photographs caused Gabrielle to scowl hard. Jordan Jacobs was the first man she'd ever taken seriously. They'd met during their residencies at M. D. Anderson Hospital in the Texas Medical Center. She'd been very leery of him in the beginning, but he'd worked on her until he'd finally convinced her to go out with him. He'd made it a point to tell her she could trust him. Their relationship was off and on for nearly a year. It had been as rocky as any rugged mountain terrain. Tristan trying to get Marjorie to trust him in the same way Jordan had gotten her to trust him had reminded her of the worst times of her life.

Tears rolled unchecked down Gabrielle's cheeks. Jordan had hurt her deeply, nearly making her lose faith in herself and every other man she came into contact with. He'd gotten her to trust him, then he'd done everything possible to make her completely lose faith in him. There'd been a time when she had believed she'd never again trust her heart to a man.

As Gabrielle had matured, she'd claimed a good portion of the blame for what had happened. Her first mistake had been in not following her strong instincts about Jordan in the first place. Natural instincts were everything.

Gabrielle now always listened for that little voice whispering in her ear. It made her think clearly and also helped direct her toward the right path. Because of what had happened with her and Jordan she did her best to steer clear of all hazardous, baggage-ridden men. Love and labor never worked. It wasn't a good match.

Perhaps I'll feel differently someday. I'd certainly like to.

The coffeemaker had beeped several minutes ago, but lost in her once painful thoughts of the past, Gabrielle had ignored it. Another glance at the clock reminded her that she had to get a move on. She still had to put on her makeup, comb her hair and dress for her first day on the job.

Cameron looked up as Gabrielle skidded into the room and tripped on the mat in front of the door. Standing behind the clinic's nursing station, located on zero level of the ship, he tried to assess what had caused her to nearly fall to the floor. Once he saw she'd kept her footing, he laughed. "Good morning, Dr. Grinage. What's your rush? You're hardly late."

Gabrielle grinned. "I wanted to make it here early, but I got caught up in something. Thank you for breakfast. It was a really thoughtful gesture."

Cameron breathed a sigh of relief, thrilled that she was okay with his surprise. "It was another way for me to welcome you. I promise not to make a habit of deciding what you eat. You're all grown up. However, I took pleasure in ordering breakfast for you this morning."

"It was a nice surprise, Dr. Cameron. I'm assuming official titles are used in the clinic."

"Just around the patients. All staff members are on a first-name basis. Many of them refer to me as Dr. Q or plain old Q. I won't be surprised if they start calling you Dr. G. Hmm, it even has a nice ring to it."

Gabrielle chuckled then looked around. "Are we the only two here?"

"It's just a matter of minutes before the others file in. There's only one staffer who has a problem with punctuality." He laughed. "I'll let you pinpoint who it is on your own."

Gabrielle smiled. "I'll try." She looked around. "I was given a brief tour of the clinic when I came aboard. I probably should walk around again and check out everything. Is that okay?"

"Fine by me," he said. "I've got the coffeemaker going. If you want a cup, it'll be ready in a couple of minutes or so."

"I've already had my two-cup limit. The coffee that room service delivered was delicious. It prompted me to brew another cup. I may've gotten spoiled."

"Room service coffee *is* excellent. Once you finish your tour, I'd like to go over the medical supplies we keep in stock. The nurses reorder all supplies, but there are occasions when doctors have to do it. We'll also go over the proper handling of various controlled medications."

"I don't think it'll take me long to get the hang of things." She turned to walk away, only to turn around. Reaching into her purse, she pulled out the book she'd promised him. "Here's the book. No hurry in returning it."

"Thanks," he said, watching after her retreating form.

Seemingly of their own volition, his smoky eyes widened, locking onto the swaying of her luscious hips. He could only define it as poetry in motion. The uniform pants were a perfect fit and beautifully outlined her seductive attributes. He found her fine body to be irresistible. Cameron mentally scolded himself on his wayward thinking and quickly returned his attention to his work.

As predicted, all but one of the other employees filed into the clinic at the same time. The habitually late crewmember was not among them. He gave his staff a big smile and a cheerful good morning.

"As some of you know, we've been expecting a new physician. Dr. Gabrielle Grinage arrived yesterday and is on duty now. For those who didn't meet her during orientation, you'll get the opportunity to do so today. She's currently touring the facility. Would anyone like to join her?"

Three new female staffers raised their hands. The two veteran employees, Morris Carey and Dean Anderson, didn't show much enthusiasm one way or the other. Meeting the newly arrived doctor didn't seem uppermost on their agenda.

Cameron knew exactly where the guys' heads were when they headed straight back to the break/lunch room, where the aroma of fresh coffee had summoned them. "Ladies, I plan to speak with each of you in an informal meeting." It was his normal procedure to speak to new crewmembers individually. "I'll take a half an hour or so with each of you. But for now, I'll take you back to meet Dr. Grinage. Did you get a chance to do any exploring on the ship last evening?"

Nurse Candi Simmons smiled broadly. "I can't believe the size of this ship. I know I haven't seen the half of it, but I'm eager to explore the entire thing."

"Good for you," Cameron remarked. "How about you, Carolyn?"

Carolyn Jackson clapped her hands enthusiastically. "Candi, Joanie and I hung out together last night. We plan to see everything during our free time."

Joanie Caldwell shook her head in disbelief. "I was so overwhelmed by the experience. I know we're here to work, but I'm also looking forward to playtime."

"Ah, playtime," Cameron remarked. "You'll get enough hours off for that."

Gabrielle took a thorough inventory of two of three good-size treatment rooms. She mentally charted the lay of each one and wrote lots of notes on a pad she'd picked up off her desk. Locked metal cabinets appeared to be chock-full of supplies. Large pieces of sterilized medical equipment had been stored away for easy access. Everything appeared pristine. There was a sterile scent in the treatment cubicles and lab areas, but it wasn't anything out of the ordinary.

She turned around when she heard a noise behind her. Seeing Cameron and three relatively young women, she smiled. "Are these lovely ladies a part of your staff?"

"*Our* staff," Cameron corrected. "They arrived the same day as you." He then introduced her to the three nurses scheduled for duty five days out of the seven.

"Once all employees are in house, I plan to have a short staff meeting with each new nurse. You're welcome to sit in if you'd like."

Gabrielle glanced at the large wall clock. "Shouldn't everyone be here by now?"

Cameron shrugged, raising an eyebrow. "Recall my earlier comment?"

Just as the words left Cameron's mouth, a man appeared in the doorway. "Morning. Sorry I'm late. That darn alarm clock in my cabin gives me fits."

"Maybe you should consider getting a new one," Gabrielle said in a no-nonsense tone. She stepped forward and extended her hand. "I'm Dr. Gabrielle Grinage. Nice to meet you. Since I feel at a disadvantage here, what's your name?"

He shook Gabrielle's hand. "I'm Joseph Clark, a nurse and senior member of the crew."

Coffee mugs in hand, nurses Morris and Dean walked into the treatment cubicle.

Cameron moved to the center of the room. "Now that we're all here, we can welcome our new staff members. I present Dr. Gabrielle Grinage, second in command, and our three newly assigned registered nurses, Joanie Caldwell, Candi Simmons and Carolyn Jackson."

The group acknowledged each other politely. Gabrielle made a mental note to get to know the individual work ethics of the nurses.

Cameron gestured toward the three men. "Nurses Morris and Dean have been with us well over a year. Joseph is a two-and-a-half-year veteran staff member.

Everyone will get to meet during our regular staff meeting at the end of the week."

Gabrielle walked around and shook everyone's hand. "I'm happy to be assigned to this ship and its clinic, and I'm looking forward to working with each of you. I'll probably ask questions of the veterans every now and then, so I'd appreciate your help."

"No problem," Joseph said. The other two male nurses nodded.

The front-desk buzzer interrupted the informal gathering.

"I'll take care of it," said Joseph, hurrying from the room.

To see how the front desk was run, Gabrielle excused herself. She made her way out to the front, where she quietly observed a middle-aged woman writing her name on the patient intake sheet. She listened closely to Joseph as he asked her reason for coming into the clinic.

The woman's hand went to her stomach. "I have nausea like you wouldn't believe. I can't keep anything down."

"How long have you been nauseated?" Joseph queried.

"It started right after lunch yesterday, even before we sailed. It may've been caused by a slice of cheesecake I ate for dessert. As soon as I finished it, I got sick."

Joseph had the patient sit down in one of several chairs lined against the wall opposite the front desk. He walked over and took her temperature and blood pressure. Nausea was a normal occurrence among passengers and the number one problem the clinic dealt with.

Gabrielle continued to watch Joseph work in an expedient manner. She liked his warm, professional de-

meanor. She'd noticed the concerned look on his face
when the cheesecake had been mentioned. Nausea
was a relatively simple problem unless it was related
to food poisoning, then it could impact a large number of guests.

Joseph went over to Dr. Grinage to consult with her
in private.

"Give her antinausea medicine and recommend she
consume only clear liquids for the next twenty-four
hours. She should also take it easy and report back to
the clinic if the symptoms continue."

No sooner had the first patient of the morning left
the clinic than several more passengers came in with
a variety of ailments. Traffic continued to flow into
the treatment center, and the staff found themselves
running from one cubicle to another. For the next few
hours, there wasn't an opportunity for anyone to take
even a short break, let alone take time for Cameron to
speak with the new personnel.

At 2:15 p.m. the clinic finally closed for lunch, which
was a good bit of time after the normal closing at one
o'clock. The clinic doors would reopen at 3:00 p.m. regardless, and Cameron and Joseph would be the on-
call staff.

Seated at the dining table in her suite later that night,
Gabrielle dined on a delicious bowl of vegetable soup
and a chicken salad sandwich. Instead of calling room
service before leaving the clinic for the day, she had prepared her own meal from the groceries and deli items
she had stocked. It had become a very busy shift at the
clinic, and passengers had come in up until the last few
minutes before closing time.

Glad that the workday was over, she planned to lie down for a while after finishing her meal. If she hadn't gotten up so early and had slept properly last night, she probably wouldn't have been so drowsy. Clinic visits had gotten hectic, with one person after another trooping in for medical care. The fast-paced day had her feeling slightly fatigued. No matter how busy the clinic had gotten, Gabrielle was thankful that no life-threatening situations had occurred.

Despite how busy the staff had become, Gabrielle had gotten an opportunity to learn quite a bit about the job throughout the shift. Cameron had been very clear in explaining to her proper patient-care procedures and had been very specific about the proper way to store and secure narcotics and other controlled substances.

After washing the few dishes she'd used, Gabrielle went into the bedroom and slipped out of her uniform. She removed from her belt the new cell phone Cameron had handed to her, informing her that she was required to have it turned on whenever the clinic was closed, even if she wasn't on call. If extra manpower was needed, she'd be alerted.

Gabrielle hastily slipped on an attractive one-piece navy blue bathing suit she'd pulled from a drawer and went out onto the balcony. She positioned her body comfortably on the chaise and tilted her face toward the sun for a few moments. Once she had gotten into a comfortable resting position place, she set the alarm on her watch.

The moment she closed her eyes, a vision of Cameron appeared. Dressed only in dark swim trunks, he looked as good as any professional athlete she'd ever seen. To have those hard, muscled arms wrapped around her would be a fantasy fulfilled. Unknowingly, Cameron was pulling Gabrielle into his white-hot web of desire, making her want him despite all the consequences.

Seated in the leather chair behind his desk, Cameron was alone in the clinic. He hadn't eaten a full breakfast, yet it had completely satisfied him. He actually fasted one day a week, drinking only liquids. The ritual had nothing to do with religion but had just started in college, when he'd pledged a fraternity, and he carried it on during his U.S. Navy duty.

Hearing a noise out front, Cameron stood. He quietly listened for more movement. It was a little early for the staff to report for duty, but it wasn't overly unusual.

With a bright smile on her face, Gabrielle popped into Cameron's office and presented him with a colorful *Thank you* balloon.

"Hi, Cameron. How's it going?"

"Great. Everything has been quiet. I wasn't called a single time last night. I came in early to work on a special report. How was your evening?"

"It was good. I ate first then stretched out on the balcony chaise and caught a few rays." Her hand went up to her face. "Did I get any darker?"

Cameron laughed heartily. "No visual changes, sorry. Come on in and have a seat."

Gabrielle grinned. "I think I will. Thank you." She sat in a chair facing him.

"I think you did great on your first day, Gabrielle. How do you think it went?"

"Fantastic. I learned quite a lot. I know the sign-in

process and where we get the paperwork for the patients to fill out. Learning the entire system may take me a while, but it'll come with time."

"The hardest thing for me to get the hang of is the billing system, though it's not a part of my job description," said Cameron. "But as the man in charge, I like to know everything there is to know about running the clinic. I do feel bad, though, when passengers have to incur extra expenses for medical reasons, so I'm glad we don't charge to treat nausea and seasickness."

"One hundred and fifty dollars to see a physician can really put a damper on vacation money," Gabrielle said.

Cameron nodded. "I hear you. Running the infirmary is expensive. It just can't be done for free. There are items we don't charge for, though." He began to feel that his remarks may be inappropriate. "I probably shouldn't be talking about this, but it does get under my skin."

Cameron thought about the number of patients he'd seen break down and cry when they were handed a large bill to sign, after being told the medical fees would be charged to their credit card.

The conversation was halted between Gabrielle and Cameron when they heard the rest of the staff reporting for duty. The two doctors walked out into the reception area to let the others know they were there. As the crew stood around making small talk and working on their assigned tasks at the same time, patients began to walk through the doors.

The clinic once again became a flurry of activity. Within minutes every staff member available was attending a patient.

After taking the blood pressure of one passenger, Gabrielle frowned. "Have you been diagnosed with high blood pressure or hypertension? If so, how long ago was it?"

"High blood pressure," the older man responded. "I was diagnosed several years ago."

Gabrielle perused the name of his medicines from the medical history. "Have you been taking your blood pressure medication?"

"I went off and left it at home," he confessed with regret.

Gabrielle held up one finger. "Give me a minute. I'll be right back."

She found Cameron in one of the treatment rooms and politely asked him to step out. Once he had followed her into the hall, she handed him the medical record and explained the medication issue.

Cameron glanced over the chart. "It's a regular stock item. Give him enough doses to last him the duration of the cruise. One of the nurses will issue him an invoice and receipt." Cameron paused. "If you don't have plans for dinner, I'd love to have you join me in my cabin."

Gabrielle managed not to blush. *Should she or shouldn't she?*

"I'd really like that." She smiled softly. "Thanks, Cameron." She popped her head into the treatment room and made eye contact with his patient. "Sorry for the interruption, ma'am."

After reaching the front desk, Gabrielle informed Morris and Candi of Cameron's order. "He'll need enough meds to last him through disembarkation. I'll

write up the medical chart, sign it and return it for billing." Without further comment, she went back to her
patient.

Back in her suite, seated on the sofa, Gabrielle couldn't
get her shoes off quickly enough. As comfortable as her
sneakers were, her feet still ached. She was used to standing for hours on end, but all the rapid moving about she'd
done inside the clinic had aggravated the soles of her feet.
It was nothing that a good soak wouldn't take care of.

She felt extremely good about her first and second
workday. Everything had run rather smoothly for her.
She hadn't encountered a single problem that she hadn't
handled easily.

Cameron had paid her a high compliment after closing hours. He had sincerely praised her on a job well
done and it had made her smile. The other new crewmembers had also received votes of confidence—he
was clearly pleased with their admirable job perfor-
mances.

Dr. Quinn was a boss who made sure his staff's morale was up. However, Gabrielle was kind of surprised
that he hadn't already tackled the issue of Joseph's late-
ness. Wondering why he'd put it off for so long, she
planned to ask him about it.

Gabrielle was delighted that Cameron had invited her
to have dinner with him in his cabin. Perhaps he wanted
them to become better acquainted as coworkers. To
think he had any romantic notions about her was probably a bit premature and even arrogant. She now knew
that he was indeed her next-door neighbor. With their
balconies side by side, Gabrielle had an idea it could get

pretty interesting under certain circumstances. Romantic notions or not, she couldn't have been more excited about dining with Cameron in his cabin. The evening would be very stimulating any way she looked at it.

Chapter 3

Gabrielle had dressed very carefully for the evening. She wore a curve-hugging navy dress and strappy sandals. Her hair hung loose again, but this time she pinned one side back with a decorative pin. She caught a glimpse of herself in the mirror inside Cameron's suite, but she was more focused on how he looked.

It was always hard for her to keep her eyes off him. He looked amazing in a pair of Calvin Klein jeans. The short-sleeved black polo shirt he wore was trimmed in white on the sleeves and collar and fitted to a tee his broad chest and ironclad muscles. On his feet he wore a pair of casual leather sandals in black.

The furnishings in his suite were very different from hers. Not only was the room much larger, Gabrielle considered his quarters to be more plush. As he *was* the commander, she understood why his accommodations were well above standard.

Cameron opened a bottle of red wine and set it on the beautifully decorated table. Besides the Wedgwood place settings and crystal stemware, colorful silk flowers nested in a wicker basket. Several unscented votive candles burned in frosted, square-shaped holders. Soft music drifted from overhead speakers. She couldn't help but be affected by the cozy, romantic atmosphere he had created.

Right after he'd entered his cabin from a hard day's work, Cameron had called guest services, which handled all special requests from employees who held key positions. Crewmembers in high profile positions received special treatment.

Cameron had placed an order for a couple of different pasta entrées, along with fresh garden salads and a variety of hot dinner rolls. It was just a matter of minutes before delivery time.

Gabrielle looked impressed with his skills. "The table looks lovely. I love the silk flower centerpiece and the votive candles."

"Thank you. My mother made the centerpiece. She's very creative with her hands and loves dabbling in arts and crafts. She and my father indulge in lots of fun classes and outings, and they also sign up for group trips for seniors."

"Mrs. Quinn knows her stuff when it comes to arranging flowers. It's good for couples to take creative classes together and socialize with folks they have something in common with. It tends to spice up the marriage. I remember when my mom and dad enrolled in Pilates at a local spa."

There was a knock on the door, and Cameron excused himself.

As he scurried across the room, Gabrielle trained her eyes on his fine physique, wondering what it'd be like to be wrapped up in his strong arms. Just imagining herself in his arms had her gulping hard.

Cameron opened the door and warmly greeted the waiter. He then stepped aside to allow him to push through the doorway a table with two trays on it and an array of other items.

The waiter busied himself setting out the food, including desserts, which consisted of thick wedges of chocolate cake with double fudge icing and two slices of baked apple pie. Once the waiter transferred everything to Cameron's table, he wished the couple a good evening and rapidly departed.

Cameron pulled out a chair for Gabrielle, which was to the left of the head of the table. "Let's eat while everything is piping hot." He smiled knowingly, hoping she'd approve of another surprise he'd arranged for her.

Gabrielle sniffed the air, appreciating the delicious smell. "I'm all for that."

For the first few minutes the couple ate in silence, each savoring the delicious taste of spaghetti simmered in marinara sauce, mixed with thin slices of zucchini and asparagus cuts. Each entrée had been cooked to perfection.

Gabrielle lifted her head and looked at Cameron. "This is the best pasta I've ever eaten. The marinara sauce is divine. I can't believe it comes from room service."

Cameron grinned. "I made a special request to guest services, which is a different department. Have you read up on all the amenities available to you?"

Gabrielle shook her head. "Not really. There's so

much stuff to read and very little time to get it done. Can you share some of what you know?"

"I'd love to," he said. "There are some wonderful amenities, such as free spa treatments and membership in the athletic club. As doctors, we get many special entitlements, but they vary depending on the status of your position. Since I'm a medical commander, my civilian ranking is higher than that of a staff physician. And your position as a senior physician is also higher than a staff physician, but not quite the same as mine. But the ranking is mostly based on work experience."

Gabrielle laughed. "I'd better get back to reading my manuals. The way these standings are handled can create a bit of controversy. Holding one position in higher esteem than another doesn't seem fair."

Cameron shrugged. "I don't make the policies, Gabrielle. I merely use the ones most beneficial to me. After you're on staff for a while, you'll understand the method to the madness. Let's face it, our jobs require more out of us than most."

"I can agree with that," she conceded.

"We sure as hell worked hard enough to get where we are. Just try to enjoy the perks you've earned. Practicing medicine can also be a thankless job. Some patients have no compunction about giving us hell."

She shrugged. "Maybe I'm a little too defensive."

Gabrielle continued eating, but she couldn't stop thinking about what he'd said. It seemed hypocritical to pit employees against each other based on professions.

With his eyes riveted on Gabrielle, Cameron took a sip of wine, which wouldn't have much effect on him, since he was already intoxicated by the beauty of the woman seated at his table. "You'll have a few hours free when we dock in Nassau. Do you plan to get off the ship?"

She lifted an eyebrow. "I sure hope to. I've read brochures on the ports we'll make and I'd like to check them out. Are you going ashore?"

Cameron relaxed back in his seat. "It depends on what's happening in the clinic at the time. There are a lot of great shops close to the dock, so I normally run around the area and pick up whatever I need during lunch. I've already explored the *Parisian Paradise*'s ports of call."

Her eyes widened with excitement. "I bet they're fascinating! I want to see the white beaches and sorbet-colored buildings I read about. And I'd love to sample the local food."

"Good choices. If I can swap a couple of hours with someone else, I'll show you around. We'll hire a cab because we won't have time for full tours. If I get the opportunity to go ashore, we can't go too far afield."

"Understood." She giggled. "I'm excited. I just might have my own personal tour guide, the amazing Dr. Cameron Quinn. Can it get any better than this?"

Cameron laughed at her teasing remarks. "Go ahead and have your fun at my expense. I have pretty thick skin, Dr. Grinage." He liked seeing her enjoying herself.

When Gabrielle had giggled like a schoolgirl, he'd found it enchanting. Her sparkling personality made him wish he could spend more time in her company. *If spending time with her wasn't so dangerous...* He purposely killed further thoughts. He simply couldn't afford to indulge in fantasies. Having her invading his dreams was bad enough.

* * *

As soon as dinner was finished, Cameron got to his feet. "Why don't you have a seat on the sofa? I'll clear the table then join you. We can eat our dessert whenever you're ready."

Gabrielle nodded. "That's fine with me." She pushed her chair back and got up. Helping him clear the table crossed her mind, but she thought better of it. He hadn't asked for assistance.

Instead of taking a seat, Gabrielle walked over to the balcony door and just stood there, peering out into the darkness. The only thing that could be seen was the brilliant show of lights in the sky. As she thought about the length of time she'd be away from home, she realized how much she would miss her family.

Five months was a long time not to see her loved ones, but being away would be longer and lonelier without a significant other. After Jordan, she hadn't dated seriously. Although she was a survivor and quickly adapted to new circumstances, she hated loneliness.

Gabrielle gave thought to Cameron's balcony right next to hers. The solid wall between the two spaces kept prying eyes at bay, but she wondered how he'd react if he somehow saw her sunning in the nude. The balconies were private enough to accommodate nude sunbathing, and her body loved to drink in the sun.

Cameron walked up behind her but kept a fair amount of space between them. "What are you thinking?"

Gabrielle decided to shock him with the truth. "How much I love to sunbathe naked."

"Me, too." He swallowed hard, fighting off an image

of her naked body. "I like feeling the sun on my body, but I'm careful not to overdo it."

"The sun feels awesome, though." She felt hot color rise in her cheeks, relieved that she wasn't facing him. Her expression would've shown her embarrassment even though she was the one who'd picked the intimate topic.

"I guess I can take that to mean you indulge in sunbathing in your birthday suit?"

"You guessed right." She tossed her head back and looked up at him.

Cameron inched his way a little closer to her. He would have liked nothing better than to wrap his arms around her from behind and rest his chin atop her head. Catching a whiff of her scent, he inhaled deeply. She smelled like the sweet, exhilarating perfume from gardenia blossoms.

To keep from backing up into him and guiding his arms around her waist, she moved away and sat down on the sofa. The strong chemistry between them felt almost flammable. As sweat formed between Gabrielle's breasts, she became hot and bothered. A cold shower would do nothing to calm the singeing heat she felt.

If he touched her, she knew her body would melt from the fiery contact. As he'd pointed out things to her in the clinic, she'd noticed his hands. He had long, lean fingers—and she was positive they knew their way around a woman's body.

Cameron took a seat on the sofa, but he again didn't get too close. Fighting his physical desire for Gabrielle was more than a battle. She had more sex appeal than any one woman should lay claim to. Keeping his distance was the only way to counter his strong desire for her. "Are you missing your family?"

Gabrielle pursed her lips. "Of course I do, but not to the point of misery. My family has always lived in the same city, but I've been away from home plenty of times."

"Mom and Dad wish I'd put down roots in one place. They hope I'll return to Houston for good, but I haven't been able to promise that. I'm like a nomad. I love to wander to distant places and foreign lands."

Gabrielle sighed. "Your bio said that you love world travel. I'll eventually go back to Galveston and practice medicine in the same communities my parents once worked in."

"What does your boyfriend think of you taking a medical post on a cruise ship?"

"He doesn't." Gabrielle hoped he didn't delve any deeper into the subject of a boyfriend; she was content to just leave it at that. She had no desire to talk about the nonexistence of a man in her life. Discussing her previous relationships would no doubt evoke some degree of pain.

Gabrielle could tell by Cameron's expression that her reluctance to talk about her love life hadn't been lost on him. Thinking it was best for her to go, she stood. She didn't want things to get too personal. Leaving was a good way to avoid it.

Cameron's on-call cell phone rang and he rapidly removed it from his belt. "Dr. Quinn."

To give him privacy, Gabrielle got up and wandered back to the balcony door.

"Cabin 1063, right away," he assured the caller, his brow furrowed with concern.

He put his phone away and walked over to her. "Gabrielle, there's an emergency. Chest pains. I need you to assist me. Please get the crash cart and portable EKG machine from the clinic and meet me in cabin 1063, tenth deck, starboard side. Bring supplies for blood and urine samples and also bring several nitroglycerine tabs."

"Right away," Gabrielle responded.

Glad she had transferred the clinic keys to her evening purse, Gabrielle rushed from Cameron's cabin and headed for the elevators. This was her first shipboard emergency and she hoped it'd go well.

Gabrielle arrived at cabin 1063 in mere minutes. As a precautionary measure, the first thing Cameron had the patient do was place a nitroglycerine tablet under his tongue. For the third time, he put his stethoscope to the passenger's bare chest and listened intently to his heart. He then rechecked his lungs. Both organs sounded distress free.

Gabrielle administered the EKG. Once the test was completed, Cameron read the results.

"Mr. Gates, what did you have for dinner?" Cameron asked. The man's heart was healthy and Cameron had determined it wasn't responsible for his chest discomfort.

The older man rattled off what he'd eaten in the dining room. Without any prompting from Cameron, he went on to say what he'd had for breakfast, lunch and snacks.

"I'm not a spring chicken, but I live an extremely active lifestyle. Overeating at every meal is pretty much the norm for me. I'm a big guy with a voracious appetite," Mr. Gates said.

Mrs. Gates hadn't said a word since she'd said hello at the door. Cameron noticed how pinched her face looked. She appeared worried, anxious and tired. He wished he could reassure her about her husband's health, but he couldn't, not until he had final results.

Cameron frowned. "Your fatty diet tells me a lot, sir. This problem may very well be a bad case of indigestion, but we can't be certain. Gastritis can produce severe chest pains, mimicking signs of a heart attack. I'd like to take blood and urine samples to complete testing. We must err on the side of caution. Think you can give us a urine sample?"

Mr. Gates shrugged. "I can."

Gabrielle stepped forth and handed him a plastic bag with a sample urine kit. "We'll draw your blood when you return."

Mr. Gates looked closely at Gabrielle. "You look mighty young. In fact, you both do. But I hear that young doctors are up on the latest in medical research, so I don't mind."

Cameron and Gabrielle smiled with understanding. They knew that young doctors were often questioned and challenged by older patients. Some elderly people preferred a well-seasoned physician, the older the better. Nevertheless, Cameron and Gabrielle were relieved that this patient felt comfortable.

Cameron took time to pack up the testing supplies while he waited for Mr. Gates to return to the room, grateful that the crash cart hadn't been necessary. Mrs. Gates still looked stressed out. He hoped he'd be able to speak with her soon to share good news.

Out of earshot of Mrs. Gates, Gabrielle conferred with Cameron. "Do you think indigestion is more than likely our diagnosis?"

He shrugged. "Too early to call, but it's feasible. His heart rhythms are steady and strong. The EKG was negative and his blood pressure is only slightly elevated. We still have to go through all the motions to make sure we get it right. We're far out at sea and the ship won't dock for another full day."

Gabrielle briefly placed her hand on Cameron's upper arm. "We've drawn the same conclusions. I noticed you didn't order blood gases."

Cameron frowned. "I didn't want to go to the extreme with a negative EKG and the absence of erratic heartbeats. Once his blood is drawn, we'll do STAT testing in the clinic."

Inside the clinic, Gabrielle brewed coffee while Cameron set up the equipment for testing the samples they'd collected. He truly believed indigestion was the culprit, but he had to be sure.

This passenger needed to reduce his fat intake, regardless, but he'd gotten the impression that sound medical advice would simply fall on deaf ears.

This man loved to eat and had proudly told how much and how often he ate. Cameron had already decided which medications he'd prescribe to treat Mr. Gates if a gastro diagnosis was confirmed.

While Cameron waited for the test results, Gabrielle returned to the lab with two plastic cups of coffee. She set both cups on a nearby shelf. "There's some coffee over here for you when you can take a break."

"I may as well drink it now while I'm waiting for the results. Is it black?"

"I saw how you take your coffee. I pay close attention to detail, remember?"

He grinned. "You're good at that. You catch on easy. I like that about you, Gabrielle."

"Do you remember how I take mine?"

"Two packets of artificial sweetener and a dry or liquid creamer." Sure that he'd gotten it right, he looked proud of himself.

She looked surprised that he actually knew the answer. "You keep on impressing me."

"It's not that big of a deal. Like you, I pride myself on paying attention." He walked over to the shelf and picked up the cup of coffee and took one quick swig. "Not bad. Maybe we should make you the official coffeemaker."

"That'd be great if I went to school for eight years just to make coffee."

"Just kidding, Gabrielle."

Her smile was flirtatious. "Nothing to forgive, Cameron. I can take a joke or two."

The completion alarm sounded on one of the testing devices. Cameron set down his cup and went to retrieve the readout. Gabrielle followed along behind him.

As Cameron took his time to decipher the urine result, he smiled knowingly. "The urine test is fine. If the blood comes back okay, I'll treat him for a gastrointestinal problem and recommend he see a gastroenterologist when he gets home."

"Good idea. Are you going back to their cabin to give them the results?"

"In this case, since it's good news, a phone call will do. Then we can get out of here."

Gabrielle stifled a yawn. "If you don't mind, I'd like to leave now. I'm pretty tired."

"Okay. I'll see you in the morning. Are you sure you'll be fine getting back alone?"

She laughed at his remark. "I come to work by myself and I was alone when I retrieved the equipment and supplies. Don't worry. I know how to get back to my cabin."

"You can't fault a guy for trying." Cameron chuckled. "Thanks for the help. Good night."

"Good night," she said, as she rushed out of the door.

Cameron hid his disappointment. He'd hoped they could continue their evening, but the emergency had interfered.

Gabrielle felt like kicking herself as she paced the floor in her cabin. It wasn't even nine o'clock, yet she'd given up on extending their evening. The first part of it had gone so well. And what had he meant by saying 'you couldn't fault a guy for trying'? *Trying what?*

Cameron's earlier mention of a boyfriend had set her teeth on edge and it shouldn't have. She hated talking about her heartbreaking experience because it just seemed plain crazy to keep rehashing the painful details.

A man who was all into himself would never be able to give enough attention to anyone else. After it had all been said and done, she had eventually come to the realization that she hadn't been in love with Jordan. In fact, she had disliked him and his deceitful ways immensely.

She quickly made up her mind to just tell Cameron about the bad experience and get it out of the way. It wasn't like they'd ever have a love connection anyway. An attraction, yes, but that was its final destination, no matter how hot the chemistry sizzling between them.

The phone rang and Gabrielle just stared at it for several seconds, wondering who was on the other end of the line. She didn't want to respond, but she had to. Although it wasn't her on-call cell ringing, it still could be a call for help. She reached for the phone's receiver and picked it up. "Hello."

A couple seconds of silence ensued. "It's Cameron. Are you okay? You left the clinic so abruptly. Is something wrong?"

The lump in her throat wouldn't go away, no matter how hard she swallowed. Cameron sounded sincere and she had to find a way to let him know it wasn't his fault.

"I'm just tired. Don't blame yourself for anything." She thought about what she'd promised herself she'd do.

Was now the right time?

She cleared her throat, hoping her voice didn't sound weak. "Listen, Cameron, let me get a bit of my past out of the way. I was once hurt very badly by someone I thought cared about me, and it took me a long time to realize that I hadn't really loved him. You asking me about a boyfriend made me revisit the past, and the memories upset me. But I'll answer your question now. I'm not involved with anyone. Plain and simple, I don't have a boyfriend."

It's out. I've come clean. It's up to him to believe me or not.

"Sorry I upset you. I hope I can make it up to you. I'd love to hang out for another hour or so. No pressure, I promise. Is coming to your cabin right now bad timing?"

Gabrielle smiled. "Your timing couldn't be more perfect. I'll be waiting."

Cameron smiled broadly. "Good. I'll be there in a jiffy."

With a big smile on her face, Gabrielle opened the door for Cameron. "I'm glad we're continuing our evening. Sorry I almost ended it."

His forefinger briefly caressed her cheek. "Don't sweat it. We all have history that causes pain or a past we're not proud of. I've been involved in an emotional breakup, so I know what it's like." He handed her a foil-wrapped package. "It's the desserts we didn't eat earlier."

"Thanks." Gabrielle put the baked goods on the kitchen counter then came back and sat on the sofa. She wanted to ask him more about his breakup, but she quickly decided not to. Just as his query had caused her to reflect on her painful past, he could experience the same emotions.

He took a seat next to her. This time he didn't make an issue of distance. "Your expression tells me you have a lot of questions. I bet you're too polite to ask me about my bad breakup, so I'll just tell you the story."

Cameron was quiet for several seconds, then he sighed hard.

"Falling for Amanda Abraham was one of the biggest mistakes of my life," he confessed. "She's a physician I worked in the same medical group with."

Cameron went on to tell Gabrielle that Amanda was

a beautiful woman who loved to openly flirt with men. Even after they'd supposedly become exclusive, her appetite for male attention didn't diminish. He had eventually learned from her that she'd been on the rebound when they'd first met. Amanda had lived with another doctor for three years prior to dating Cameron—and then she'd gone back to her ex-boyfriend without bothering to tell him.

"Amanda's ex showed her no respect whatsoever. He constantly cheated on her and they'd had issues with domestic violence. I tried to help her, but I couldn't. I finally figured out she was into bad boys, the superbad ones." He shrugged. "I simply didn't fit the description."

Gabrielle's eyes filled with empathy. "Of course you didn't. Both women and men can get caught up in relationships with cheating and abusive tendencies. I don't get it, but they obviously do."

"I'd never mistreat anyone. I don't have a mean bone in my body. I'd rather walk away from someone than stay and hurt them."

Even though she felt the same as he did on the subject of dating, his words hit her like a ton of bricks. "You're very sweet. I picked that up about you right away. I'm sorry you were hurt."

"Thank you for saying that. But if anything, I'm too caring."

Gabrielle shook her head. "You're fine, just the way you are. Any woman who earns your respect and love should consider herself extremely lucky."

"Thanks again." Cameron smiled weakly. "You said that you really didn't love him. What's his name and why did you think you were in love?"

Gabrielle bit down on her lower lip to stop its trembling. "Dr. Jordan Jacobs did everything he could to get me to trust him. Once I did, he gave me every reason not to."

As she explained to Cameron what a jerk Jordan had turned out to be, she surprisingly released some things she didn't know she still held inside. Anger was an emotion she had a hard time dealing with. She'd been taught to never carry rage to bed or into the next day. Her parents had taught her to work through her pain reasonably and to never let it fester within.

"Your parents sound wise. Anger isn't something I give in to easily, either. It takes a lot to get me there. My back has to be literally against the wall," Cameron said.

"I'm not an angry person, either, but Jordan could make my blood boil. Unlike Amanda, I didn't allow anyone to disrespect me. At least, I thought I didn't. My biggest problem is that I'm a sore loser. And I'm not a quitter. I stayed around as long as I did because I didn't want to concede defeat. I hate feeling like a failure, but it was Jordan who had failed."

Cameron fought the desire to take her hand. She looked so vulnerable and about ready to cry. "What eventually made you get out of the relationship?"

"It's hard to be with a guy who puts himself first all the time, yet I stayed. I got out because I realized I didn't love him. More than that, I didn't even like him. Still, I let him trample me."

Cameron's eyebrows lifted. "Trample you? I can't imagine it."

"Try to imagine people stomping grapes to make wine. Jordan stomped on me and everyone else in his path."

"But you won in the end. You kicked him hard to the curb, right?"

Gabrielle couldn't help laughing. "I embedded him in it, like it was wet concrete. Jordan realized too late that no one gets away with stomping on me. Before I'd treat him like he did me, I chose to get out."

"What did your brothers think of how you were treated?"

"You really don't want to know. My brothers possess iron fists like lethal weapons. I did Jordan one last favor. I kept my brothers off him."

Cameron and Gabrielle laughed.

Finally Gabrielle blew out a breath of relief. "I'm ready for dessert. What about you?"

"You bet. I worked up an appetite just by opening up to you then hearing your own story. If you don't mind, I'd like a slice of pie and cake."

"Coming right up." Gabrielle got to her feet. "Coffee?"

"The mug I had in the lab was the last coffee of the night for me. I rarely drink anything with caffeine this late. Do you have milk?"

Gabrielle smiled. "I'll bring you a glass. Be right back."

She placed two slices of apple pie and a wedge of chocolate cake onto a dessert plate, poured a glass of milk, then placed everything on a plastic tray and carried it over to the coffee table.

Cameron stood and took the tray from her. "Mind if we eat out on the balcony?"

"That's a great idea."

Gabrielle followed Cameron out the door and onto the balcony. She sat down on one of two chairs. The swirling trade winds were warm. It was a balmy night, a perfect evening for enjoying the outdoors. Romance was in the air, but she couldn't go there, not even in her thoughts. She had to take seriously their rules about dating coworkers. Yet thoughts of him kissing her had a near-tangible impact on her. It was as if she could feel his lips on hers.

Good luck controlling your constant, torrid thoughts of Cameron.

Taking a lighter from his pants pocket, Cameron picked up a tall candleholder from the table and lit the pillar candle inside. The yellowish-orange flame came to life, glowing brightly. He couldn't help noticing how the light had settled on her lovely face, causing it to glow also. Her angelic expression made him think she appreciated the candlelit atmosphere he'd created.

Reining in his thoughts, Cameron served the dessert dishes.

The first bite of cake tasted scrumptious to Gabrielle. "Wow! I can't help but sing praises to the pastry chef. This cake is so fresh and moist, and the fudge icing is just right."

"Glad I chose the right desserts." After taking a forkful of pie and putting it into his mouth, he moaned with pleasure. "You should try the apple pie. It's delicious."

Without thinking about it, he put more pie on his fork and held it up to Gabrielle's mouth.

The intimate gesture surprised her. Their eyes met and locked and an unexpected moment of intense passion flared between them. Cameron and Gabrielle found it difficult to break the trance they'd fallen into.

She took a bite of the offered dessert—to do otherwise might've hurt his feelings. "It's every bit as good as the cake. The crust is so light and flaky. I'll eat my slice of pie for lunch tomorrow, unless you'd like to have it. I'm more than willing to give it up. " Gabrielle bit down on her lip, wishing she could take the suggestive words back.

"One slice of pie is enough for me. I don't normally eat sweets this late," Cameron said. "But I occasionally eat a piece of fruit before I go to bed."

"I'm not a late-night eater, either," said Gabrielle.

A wild night of making love with you could change all of that, Dr. Quinn. I'd probably be ravenous for something sweet…and not just food.

Gabrielle ate the last bite of her cake. Then she felt a bit of chocolate icing lingering on her lips. As she discreetly licked it off, an immediate image of Cameron's tongue sensuously removing the frosting made her blush. She felt fiery sensations down to the tip of her toes. Turning off intimate thoughts about him wasn't easy.

Cameron picked up the glass of milk and downed it. "That hit the spot." He wiped his mouth with a napkin. "The milk was good and cold."

"I'm glad you enjoyed it. I enjoyed the dessert, but I can't do this too often. All this gourmet food at my disposal 24/7 is kind of daunting. I'll have to control my willpower."

Cameron laughed. "Or just get in plenty of exercise. The fitness center is fully equipped and has the most modern exercise equipment available. And there are times when you may be too busy to eat. I can't tell you how many times I've missed meals."

"You can always call room service," Gabrielle countered.

"Not when I'm in the middle of a case and bone tired.

Once the patient is stable, all I want to do is shower and fall into bed. Ask the veteran staff. They'll tell you. Food is never a priority for us when our passengers are in need of medical care. They come first."

"I understand. Passengers are also first on my priority list. Food will have to wait," she said soberly. She and Cameron had suddenly gotten serious, and it felt kind of awkward.

Cameron laughed. "We're coming off a bit somber all of a sudden."

Gabrielle decided to change the subject so she could learn more about the man. "I had the same thought. So…you mentioned being an only son. Are you an only child?"

Cameron grinned. "I have two beautiful older sisters. Corinne and Coral are twins."

"Nice names. I bet you're protective of them."

"They're seven years older than me. I wish I could be protective. They'd only tell me to mind my own business if I tried."

"It seems like in life women have no choice but to toughen up in mind, body and spirit. After all, there's nothing more devastating than being manhandled emotionally and physically."

Cameron tapped the side of his head. "There are all sorts of abuses in the world."

Gabrielle understood what he'd meant. "I second that."

He looked at his watch and practically jumped to his feet. "It looks like my hour is up, but I really enjoyed myself. I'm glad we talked over our personal issues. I normally wouldn't think of telling a stranger some things I shared with you." He grinned. "But I don't see you as a stranger. You're someone I'd love to have as a friend."

Gabrielle extended her hand to Cameron. "I hope you do consider us friends."

Cameron took hold of Gabrielle's hand, but instead of letting it go, he guided her inside and held her hand all the way to the front door.

His tender care of her hand made her want to throw herself into his arms and kiss him like no friend would ever dare to do. His touch was so soft and warm. Having his hands rove her body would be magical. She had a feeling he was capable of taking her places she'd never been.

She winced as Jordan's image flashed in her mind. Gabrielle hadn't been blind to his deceptions; she'd just been too immature to deal with a conniving man who had caused her excruciating pain and hadn't thought anything of it.

But there weren't any comparisons between Cameron and Jordan. Cameron was clearly the better man.

Gabrielle was jolted back to the present when Cameron's lips gently pressed against her forehead. Her eyes grew wide with wonder and surprise—and there was nothing she could do to hide it.

A hint of a smile on his lips, Cameron stared deeply into her eyes. "Thanks for a great evening. Tomorrow looks rather promising. Good night."

He stepped out into the hallway and shut the door behind him, leaving Gabrielle nearly swooning against the closed door.

Cameron's kindness, selflessness and affection had Gabrielle's emotions reeling. How much of himself would he be willing to give to her? She couldn't help but wonder.

Was it conceivable that they could get past their hurt and give in to each other? With love, wasn't everything possible?

Chapter 4

As the *Parisian Paradise* sailed into Nassau, the capital city of the Bahamas, Gabrielle marveled at the picturesque scenery from her balcony. Buildings with flashy colors and endless rows of shops appeared close enough for her to reach out and touch. Aiming her camera at the docking pier and then the shops, she snapped digital photos to store in her new travel album.

Gabrielle kept thinking back to Cameron saying he'd escort her ashore if it was possible. She was waiting on his call and hoped he had good news. Touring with him would be fun.

The infirmary staff on the *Parisian Paradise* was on call, but they took turns with coverage while others toured the ports of call, sightseeing and seeking out great shopping venues.

On the first three days at sea, plenty of passengers

had sought out some form of medical care, but nothing had been serious. There hadn't been a dull moment inside the clinic throughout its hours of operation. Gabrielle and the other new crewmembers were looking forward to the ship docking so they could get away and explore.

Gabrielle thought she looked pretty decent for someone who'd had very little sleep. By the time she had pulled a blanket up over her body last night, fatigue had already set in.

A shower and going straight to bed had been the perfect remedies. Although it was highly unusual for her to stay in bed late, she had slept until 6:30 a.m. It was now seven-fifteen, and she'd showered only minutes ago.

As Gabrielle donned a navy blue floral bikini, thoughts of going ashore had her as excited as a kid taking a first pony ride. She slipped a colorful cover-up over her swimsuit. Her beach towel was packed away in a straw satchel, along with sunscreen and various other necessities.

The phone rang and Gabrielle ran over to the bedside table. "Good morning. It's Gabrielle."

"Hey, it's Cameron. I've got coverage for a few hours. How soon can you get to the disembarkation point?"

"I can be at level zero in ten or fifteen minutes. I'm packed and about ready to go."

"Use your private employee elevator key. The corridors are packed with passengers waiting to go down to level zero. And you should make sure to wear comfortable shoes and bring along bottled water. We'll do a good bit of walking. See you soon."

After hanging up, Gabrielle ran into the kitchen and took out several bottles of water to pack in her satchel.

She'd planned to take a romance novel, but now that Cameron was escorting her, she wouldn't have time to read. Instead, she rushed into the bathroom, where she gathered her long tresses into a ponytail and secured it tightly with a white banded scarf. She locked the suite and strode down the corridor, not knowing which she was more eager for—her day in Nassau or her day with Cameron.

Gabrielle was amazed at the pristine condition of the white, sugary sand beach. After laying her towel on a chaise, she stripped off her shorts and shirt and plopped down onto it. Leaning to the left, she reached down and scooped up a handful of sand and sifted it through her fingers. "So this is Cable Beach, huh? I've read so much about it."

Cameron rubbed sunblock onto his shoulders and abdomen. "This is the famous one. It's a good thing we caught an early tender. Cable Beach gets way too crowded for my comfort. I prefer private shorelines. Luckily there's an agreement between the resorts and cruise lines for employees to have access to their entire facility. We just have to show our employee IDs."

Gabrielle smiled. "That's another nice perk. Thanks again for clueing me in."

"You'd eventually find out everything, but it's much better to get a heads-up."

"*Eventually* can use up a lot of time. I learned that the hard way." Thinking of all the wasted time it had taken her to arrive at *eventually* with Jordan made her wince.

The painful look in her eyes made him want to cheer her up. The last thing she needed was to plunge back into the past. This was a new chapter in her life, and she was on board to work and have a good time.

Suddenly, Cameron lifted Gabrielle into his arms and headed for the water. Holding her securely, he ran into the surf, laughing deeply. Warm as a summer day, the clear turquoise waters engulfed them. With her arms still around his neck, Gabrielle grinned. "If this water had been cold, you'd be in trouble."

"Glad that didn't happen. And there's no chilly water this time of year. Can you swim?" He knew he'd asked a stupid question the moment it had left his mouth.

She was both amused and annoyed at his comment. "Passing a swim test is a requirement for being hired… and you know it. All crewmembers have to know how to swim."

"You're right. I *do* know." He set her on her feet and made sure she had her balance. Holding her against him had caused his lower body to set up shop. Desire for her flared hotly and deeply inside of him. He didn't want to feel this way, and he fought the urge to kiss her.

To regain his composure, Cameron swam away from Gabrielle, kicking up a lot of white spray. Farther and farther out he swam, diving under at intervals and coming up moments later.

When Cameron didn't resurface again, a sudden bout of panic struck her. She kept her eyes trained on the distant waters, hoping he'd reappear as quickly as he'd disappeared. A minute or so later, there was still no sign of him, and she hurriedly decided to call a lifeguard.

As Gabrielle cut through the waters, rushing back to the sandy shore, she felt something go around her waist and propel her backward. Then Cameron surfaced.

When they were face-to-face he looked at her mischievously. "Scared you, didn't I?"

"No way," she protested emphatically. He was dead on, but she'd never concede.

"I'll race you back to shore."

"Not a chance. I'll leave you so far behind, you'll feel abandoned."

Gabrielle gave a loud harrumph. "You think so, huh? I'm a very strong swimmer. I won three championships in a row when I was on the relay swim team in college."

Cameron threw his head back and laughed. "Girl, you don't stand a chance in Hades of winning against me. Have you noticed how long my legs are?"

"I've noticed, but stature isn't an indication of strength." She clucked at him like a chicken. "Grow some feathers and take the challenge."

"You're on." He took off, swimming fast and hard toward the beach.

Once Gabrielle realized Cameron had actually accepted the challenge and had begun the race, she kicked her strong athletic abilities into high gear. "Girl Wonder is right on your tail," she yelled, knowing full well he couldn't hear her.

Cameron looked back and saw that he was way ahead of her. He slowed down to give her a half a chance of getting closer, but he had no intentions of letting her win. Minutes later, much to his chagrin, he realized he'd been eyeing the wrong swimmer.

Gabrielle swam completely under water. Without surfacing, she swam hard. Her lungs were as strong as her legs and arms. In shallow water now, she finally came up for air.

Raising her hand in victory, she ran the short distance to the shore and dropped down on the sand. She watched as Cameron came up out of the water looking like a chiseled marble statue. Smirking at him, she cupped her ear. "What did you say about me earlier?"

A slightly embarrassed Cameron made his way over to where Gabrielle had stretched out. Nearly out of breath, he plopped down next to her then looked at her sheepishly. "Congratulations for the win and for making a liar out of me. I could've beaten you if I had kept going, but I looked back and my eyes latched on to the wrong person."

"Could've, would've, should've," she mocked. "Save the lame excuses."

All Cameron wanted to do was take her into his arms and kiss her until she was as breathless as he was. Of all the female doctors in the world, why had one so intelligent, attractive and seductive been put in his path? Her athleticism was an added bonus. He felt more than a physical reaction to her, and it had him worried. He ached to tell her how much he wanted her, but he couldn't do that. Gabrielle was strictly off limits.

If they weren't coworkers, Cameron would've told Gabrielle about his instant attraction to her within minutes of their first meeting. Her beauty and brains made him feel alive whenever he was in her company. It was now days later—and his attraction to her had grown tenfold. There was no easy way to deal with this complicated dilemma.

Gabrielle and Cameron got out of a taxicab and hurriedly boarded a jitney to visit more island destinations.

Seated next to Gabrielle, Cameron watched her expressions of astonishment as they entered colorful

Bay Street, Nassau's busiest district. The Straw Market, countless shopping venues, restaurants and the business district were popular tourist attractions. The island's history of slavery could be found nearby at the Pompey Museum.

As the carriage slowly moved through the streets, Cameron pointed out other attractions to Gabrielle. "This area is known as Parliament Square. It's where Bahamian government buildings are located. That beauty there is a statue of Queen Victoria."

They came up on Rawson Square. Gabrielle's eyes were instantly drawn to a dominating figure. "What does the bronze statue represent?"

"It commemorates Bahamian women." He pointed out the Water Tower. "That's the highest point on Nassau. You can see the most spectacular views of the island from up there. It's actually breathtaking."

Gabriele wrapped her arms together. "I feel so relaxed. What about you?"

"I've never been uncomfortable when I'm just hanging out or shopping around. Bahamian folks are super friendly, so I always feel relaxed and welcomed here."

Gabrielle nodded. "The people *are* nice and friendly, but there are way too many vendors on Cable Beach. I was uncomfortable with how crowded it was."

"I mentioned the overcrowding to you earlier. It's a big issue for me. I normally use one of the larger hotel resorts. The Sheraton is my favorite." Cameron glanced at his watch. "We have time to get in a couple more sights. Interested in sailing the harbor in a glass-bottom boat?"

"I'd love to do that." She wrinkled her nose. "But I'm getting a bit hungry."

"Not a problem. I'll make sure you get some local food. Arawak Cay, aka Fish Fry, is a good place to eat. You should try the conch salad and fried snapper. It's superb. If you want a drink, the Daq Shack serves up the best daiquiris on the island."

She laughed. "I like the name of the place. Do they have virgin drinks? I don't want to order anything alcoholic in case I end up working."

"I don't think you'll be called in, but I know what you mean. I called the infirmary while you were in the ladies' room at the beach, and all is quiet. Most everyone is probably out here enjoying the sights and sounds of Nassau."

"Just like us. I've had a great time so far. I hope I get to go ashore in Freeport." She shrugged. "If not on this trip, I'm sure I'll get there sooner or later."

"Anything is possible. Our crew is great at accommodating each other, and we're always happy to provide coverage for new employees. I'm the man in charge so I end up staying aboard more often than not."

Gabrielle smiled softly. "That's commendable. It's what a great commander does."

Grinning, Cameron nodded. "Not all medical commanders see it as I do. I work hard to keep my crew's morale up. When they're happy, I reap the benefits of their satisfaction. I want things to go well for them, so I put their needs before my own."

"I've heard about how much your crew loves and respects you." Gabrielle rubbed her stomach when it interrupted with a growl. "Let's get some food so I can calm the protesters."

They both erupted in laughter.

* * *

Back inside her suite and freshly showered, Gabrielle was sprawled out on her king-size bed, wearing a pair of loose-fitting pink-and-black silk pajamas. Her silky chestnut hair had been brushed back and secured with a soft pink hair wrap.

Despite Gabrielle's physical and mental fatigue, she couldn't curb imposing thoughts of Cameron, who'd been a perfect gentleman from beginning to end of their Nassau excursion. They'd watched vividly colorful sea life in their natural habitat from the glass-bottom boat, and he'd been able to name all the species. His range of knowledge had left her utterly astonished.

Gabrielle had pegged Cameron as a researcher. He had to know everything there was to know on anything and everything that sparked his interest. She was pretty much the same way; she always wanted to learn all she could about anything igniting her curiosity.

To relieve the staff on duty, Cameron had reported to the infirmary immediately after they'd returned to the ship. His quick kiss to her cheek still had Gabrielle floating on a cloud. She had begun missing him the moment he'd left her side. It wasn't a good sign.

Cameron kept Gabrielle's curiosity aroused. They both had had disastrous relationships with coworkers, which made her want to keep their interactions simple. But her strong desire for this gorgeous man was so complex it defied meaning. No matter how big her crush was, Gabrielle had to find a way to keep her wild attraction under control.

Spending time alone with a hunk like Cameron was asking for trouble. But then again, she thought, friends spent time alone together. Developing a sound friendship with him was extremely important to her. Since they couldn't become lovers, being friends would at least enable her to keep him in her life in some capacity. Having him as her mentor was also a good way to keep him around. Cameron had a lot of work experience and useful knowledge under his belt, which could be helpful to her.

Repositioning the pillow under her head, she squirmed about until she regained the comfort zone she'd achieved earlier. The phone rang, and she moved away from the pillow once again to reach the receiver.

She picked up the phone, and a big smile formed on her lips. "Marjorie, how are you?"

"Good. How are things for you, Gabrielle?"

"Other than feeling a bit tired, I couldn't be better."

Other than this inferno burning inside me for Cameron, I'm fine.

"You sound happy. Dr. Quinn told me about your fun tour of Nassau. I'm glad you went ashore for a few hours."

Gabrielle didn't know what to make of Cameron telling everyone about their day.

It wasn't top secret, but was Marjorie the only one he'd told about it?

"It was…enjoyable," she stammered, knowing she'd made a gross understatement.

Visiting so many fabulous island venues had been fun and educational, but spending time with Cameron had been especially delightful.

"He's an excellent tour guide, and he's shown several of his crewmembers around. Dr. Q knows so much about the island's off-beaten paths, but he's also up on all the hot spots."

"That, he is," Gabrielle agreed. She could go on for hours singing Cameron's praises, but that wouldn't help her situation. Instead, she changed the subject. "What time do you get off?"

"My shift ends in just a few minutes. I looked at to-morrow's schedule and saw that we're on duty together, which should be fun. But I really called to see if you've made plans for this evening."

"Haven't given it any thought. I did a lot of walking today so I'll have to consult my feet. What are you in the mood for?"

"I was hoping we could have dinner together," Marjorie said. "We can do the early sitting then catch a live theater show."

"The early sitting means we'd eat in one of the formal dining rooms, but I guess I can handle it. I've been in casual clothes most of the time, so I'd like to dress up."

"Good. Do you mind if Tristan joins us?"

Gabrielle thought that perhaps that question should've been asked beforehand. "Well, I don't want to be a third wheel."

"Nonsense! Tristan loves it when you have dinner with us. If you feel that way, maybe Cameron can join us. I can invite him before he leaves the clinic. What do you think?"

"I'll leave it up to you." No way was Gabrielle going to protest anything to do with Cameron, yet she felt somewhat uncomfortable. They'd already spent several fun-filled hours together. God forbid that he'd think she'd put Marjorie up to inviting him to dinner.

"I'll see you at the Paris dining room at five forty-five. By the way, both Tristan and I are on call tonight."

"Hopefully there won't be any emergencies. Looking forward to some fun."

"Same here. See you later."

As Gabrielle cradled the phone, she couldn't help wondering if this dinner idea might be a setup by a matchmaker named Marjorie Carson. Gabrielle wouldn't put it past her to arrange a reason for her and Tristan to be called away, leaving her alone with Cameron. But according to Cameron, each time he'd called into the infirmary while ashore everything had been quiet. Maybe it'd remain that way so everyone could enjoy their evening, Gabrielle thought, as she pulled a pillow back under her head.

Gabrielle dressed carefully, pairing a fabulous beige linen form-fitting sheath with dark red patent leather shoes and a matching bag. A delicate gold chain with a single two-carat ruby caressed her throat. Tiered ruby earrings dangled from her ears.

Wearing her hair in a loose, swept-up style was a daring addition to her chic look. She'd taken a big risk by painting her full lips in red high-gloss sheen, but a look into a mirror showed her how well the daring shade highlighted her skin tone. Before leaving the cabin, Gabrielle ran into the bathroom and sprayed a delectable scent by Guerlain onto her pulse points. She had only twenty minutes to make it to her distant destination, which worried her. The Paris dining room wasn't anywhere near her suite, and she'd have to hustle quite a bit to be on time. The elevators would be crammed full with the early sitting diners, but she was lucky to have use of the employee elevators as an alternative.

Out in the hallway, Gabrielle looked over at the door to Cameron's suite.

Is he there or did he go out?

Not knowing if he had accepted or declined the dinner invitation had her nerves on edge. One minute she hoped he had accepted, and in the next instant she thought it was best if he'd given his regrets. Right now she admitted she'd be utterly disappointed if he had declined.

Walking at a brisk pace, Gabrielle made her way to the nearest employee elevator.

There was no sign of Cameron outside the Paris dining room. Gabrielle blew out a ragged breath of bitter disappointment. She told herself not to take his absence personally. As she headed over to where Marjorie and Tristan stood waiting, she quickened her pace.

The three friends exchanged hellos and warm hugs.

Marjorie briefly held Gabrielle's hand. "I'm glad you could make it. The maître d' will let us in soon, but it seems they're running a little behind schedule."

"There's no hurry," Gabrielle said.

Tristan lightly pecked Gabrielle's cheek. "It's nice to see you. You look lovely."

Gabrielle smiled. "Why thank you, Tristan. You look pretty good yourself."

Tristan grinned and nodded.

Marjorie was out of uniform, which made Gabrielle check her from head to toe. The red dress she wore was stunning and it hugged her delicate curves. She had to laugh when she saw that they wore matching colors but in the reverse.

"Cameron should be along shortly," Marjorie told

Gabrielle. "A passenger showed up in the infirmary just as he was about to lock up. He doesn't think it's anything serious."

So Cameron is joining us.

A wave of euphoria swept over Gabrielle. She struggled to successfully mask how happy she was. She felt like breaking out in song and dance, but no one could know about her deep desire for Dr. Quinn.

Although she was horribly confused about what direction their relationship might go in, she wasn't the least bit perplexed about her steadily growing romantic feelings for him. She had fallen hard for Cameron Quinn. Once they had sat in the glitzy Paris dining room, Gabrielle gazed out the ship's wall-to-wall windows, which offered great panoramic views. The sun hadn't set yet and she couldn't wait to watch it set with Cameron by her side.

Cameron strolled into the dining room, his eyes straight ahead. He was eager to get to the table where his friends sat, yet he still took time to enthusiastically greet passengers who recognized him.

There was an empty space on Gabrielle's side of the table and he sat down next to her. "Sorry I'm late. When duty calls, we answer."

In a whispery voice, Gabrielle let him know she was happy he could join them. No one had heard what she'd said to him, but her comment had come through clearly to him.

Cameron leaned into Gabrielle, putting his mouth close to her ear. "You look ravishing! Thrilled I was invited."

Gabrielle smiled radiantly. "Thank you. And you couldn't look any hotter."

Cameron's heart skipped a beat. "If you all don't want to wait for the waiter to arrive, I can get us drinks from the bar," he suggested.

"I've already ordered wine," Tristan informed him. "The waiter shouldn't be long getting back to us."

No sooner had the words left Tristan's mouth than the waiter appeared with two bottles, and he poured wine in their crystal stemware.

"I'm assuming everyone but me has looked at the menu," Cameron said, "so let me take a gander at this evening's entrées." He picked up his menu and flipped it open, but in a few seconds he set it aside again.

"That was quick," Gabrielle said. "Did you take a course in speed reading?"

Cameron's piercing eyes darkened then fastened on Gabrielle. "I'm a man who knows exactly what he wants. I don't waste time pondering."

Color crept into Gabrielle's cheeks. She knew Cameron hadn't been only talking about food choices, but it was best to let it go. Trying to figure him out was probably useless. Dr. Quinn was a multifaceted man.

As Cameron's eyes continued to devour Gabrielle, he thought about how beautiful she looked. Every man wanted a gorgeous woman who possessed a dynamic personality and a sexy body. But looks and a fabulous body weren't nearly enough to satisfy Cameron. He wanted so much more. He wanted to experience a deeper connection with his soul mate, to have more of a spiritual journey. His idea of true love was two kindred spirits united together in ways that had nothing to do with outward beauty or hot pleasures of the flesh.

If anyone could change his mind about falling for a coworker, Gabrielle was the one. From what she'd said last night, she wasn't too thrilled about dating coworkers, either. Her ordeal with her ex still pained her a lot, but he wasn't anything like Jordan. It was bad enough that he was in danger of breaking his own rules, but Cameron knew that she also had to want it for anything to occur. Yet he'd already foolishly told her he wanted her as a friend, completely omitting the romantic feelings he had for her.

What man in his right mind wanted only friendship from the woman who visited his dreams?

Cameron quietly asked himself if he would miss out on something wonderful and gratifying if he kept her at arm's length. What if Gabrielle was indeed his soul mate? Was it possible they were destined for each other? It was a mind-boggling situation.

Thoughts of them becoming romantically involved constantly taxed his mind and challenged his rule about not mixing work and women. Cameron wasn't so sure which one would eventually win out.

The party of four dug into their delicious looking meals with gusto.

Gabrielle noticed that Marjorie and Tristan were very attentive to each other. Every so often he twirled the ends of her hair around his finger. Their eyes stayed deeply connected whenever they talked.

Had Cameron not been there Gabrielle wondered if she would've felt totally out of place. She had to wonder if there was a love connection in their future. If so, would they give in to their desires for each other despite being coworkers? Cameron was the only man who'd ever made her heart beat so fast and with such meaning.

The two couples had left the Paris dining room right after dessert and had walked the short distance to the Cannes Festival Theater, where they'd watched a Broadway revue entitled *Hot Stuff.* After the show, they went to the Eiffel Tower Lounge, which was selected by the men for its variety of after-hours entertainment. The lounge had dancing, live bands, karaoke sessions, a DJ and piano bar. The venue was designed with a spacious parquet floor, and dim overhead lighting and candlelit tables created a cozy, romantic ambience.

Once Cameron claimed a table with perfect views of the entire lounge, Marjorie and Tristan excused themselves and headed straight for the dance floor.

Cameron pulled out at a chair for Gabrielle. "Would you like to dance before we settle in?"

Gabrielle nodded eagerly. "I'd love to. The steel band is smoking."

Cameron took Gabrielle by the hand and led her to the parquet floor, purposely steering clear of the area where Marjorie and Tristan were. He wanted to give the couple their privacy, and he also shamefully wanted Gabrielle to himself. He turned around and gently brought her in close. Excitement bubbled within Cameron as he held her in his arms. She had him aching badly for her.

How many times have I thought about kissing her?

He'd already lost count. Every time he fantasized about her, he wished they could be more than coworkers. When she appeared in his thoughts and dreams, he easily surrendered his full attention to her.

Cameron wanted Gabrielle as his lover, his one and

only lover. He had had a complete change of heart about dating coworkers. Everything about her was intriguing to him despite the fact they'd only met days ago, and it was hard for him to keep his eyes off her at work and during training sessions and even at play. He loved her velvety soft voice and the tender compassion she had for her crewmembers and the patients she treated.

He had never believed that one woman and one man could have it all and could do it all for each other. But Gabrielle not only had him entertaining that possibility, she had him already conceding that it was doable if he moved slowly and carefully.

The tempo of the music suddenly sped up drastically. Many guests who'd sat out the slow songs rushed to the dance floor as faster-paced music blared from every corner of the room. Gabrielle was happy she knew all the latest dance steps. Her friends at home loved to party, and dancing was one of their favorite things to do. Gabrielle and Cameron danced the first two slow songs of the next set before returning to the table. As Gabrielle looked around for Marjorie and Tristan, she couldn't spot them in the crowd.

Shortly after they took their seats, the handsome DJ stepped to the microphone.

"Greetings, ladies and gentlemen! Is everyone having a good time?" A wave of thunderous applause exploded. "Welcome to the Eiffel Tower Lounge! We're now moving into the first karaoke session of the evening. Come on up and give it a try. No need to be shy."

A very attractive woman immediately took the stage. Marjorie and Tristan reclaimed their seats just before the lady belted out the first note. "This should be a blast," Tristan remarked, rubbing his hands together in eager anticipation.

The music to Whitney Houston's "I Will Always Love You" softly swirled around the room.

As the music played, a waitress came to take drink orders from the group.

Gabrielle cleared her throat. "I'd like to have a club soda with lime."

Cameron smiled knowingly. "I'll have the same as the lady, thank you."

Marjorie and Tristan followed suit by ordering virgin drinks. Everyone had early-morning duty, not to mention the even earlier repeat lifeboat training and mandatory safety sessions. Once everyone had drinks in hand, their sights were set on center stage.

The female singer had a robust voice and did justice to the song she'd taken on. It wasn't a Whitney Houston performance, but she had excellent control of her vocals and was able to hit all the high notes and guttural lows. As she stepped down from the stage, she received a standing ovation.

"Wow! Anyone who goes onstage after her better have their act together. She was amazing," Gabrielle said.

Cameron smiled at Gabrielle. "Want to do a duet with me?"

Gabrielle drew her head back. "No way am I getting up there. I got a feeling this crowd can get fierce. The first singer knew what to do with a microphone, but what if no one else does?"

"Since you won't join me, I hope you enjoy." Cameron stood. "Wish me luck." He strode off toward the stage. Passengers and crewmembers who recognized him clapped and cheered.

Marjorie snickered. "My money is on the commander. Look at his sexy swagger. That's not the strut of a man who's about to make a fool of himself."

Gabrielle got up from her seat. "Well, I don't know what'll happen, but I'm going to join him. If he's brave enough to get up there, I'll show him I have just as much bravado. Wish us luck."

As she heard the name of the song Cameron had chosen, Gabrielle wished she could turn and run back to the table. "Where Is the Love" was a favorite, and it was a beautifully written and arranged oldie but goodie song.

Smiling broadly to show his appreciation of her support, Cameron stepped up to Gabrielle, handing her the smallest mike. Enfolding her hand in his, he held it tightly.

The first notes out of Cameron's mouth were unbelievably beautiful, making her weak in the knees. Glad the words to the song were on the prompter, she sweetly, soulfully, sang her part, showing she also had a fantastic singing voice.

They stared into each other's eyes and suddenly the performance felt very intimate and romantic. So close to swooning, Gabrielle hoped she could hold up until the song was over. From Gabrielle's and Cameron's very real flirtatious gestures, no one would've guessed they weren't madly in love. The performance brimmed with passion, and their voices blended together splendidly. She sang alto and soprano. He hit high, low and deep guttural notes, pleasantly surprising his friends and crewmembers. With their eyes locked in an impenetrable embrace, the couple tried to figure out what messages they were sending to each other.

Gabrielle knew she'd want Cameron as her lover if it weren't so complicated. *Would he want her the same way?* She and Cameron as lovers would more than likely be off the charts. She knew that if she gave in, waves of forbidden passion would sweep them out to their very own private island.

Although today was a new day and all negativity had to be squashed, she hadn't yet fully reconciled with the issue of dating a coworker. But at this moment, Gabrielle had never been happier. Life was good for her, and she silently vowed to make sure it stayed that way.

Chapter 5

Gabrielle massaged sunblock into her freshly showered skin. The sun hadn't come up yet, but she was due at the appointed muster station within the next thirty minutes for another training session. Surprised by Cameron's early-morning wakeup call, she had barely been able to contain herself. She was so attracted to him that remaining aloof in front of other employees would be difficult. Gabrielle was afraid everyone else would pick up on the electrifying chemistry between them, just like Marjorie had.

Not wanting to borrow trouble, Gabrielle had to keep her distance from Cameron as much as possible during training. Thank goodness they were in different groups, though actively a part of the same session. This was about business, and she planned to remind herself of it every second. It'd be so easy to get sidetracked because he was always on her mind.

Cameron had also informed her that he'd checked out their work schedules, and if she wanted, there'd be time for him to show her around Freeport, Bahamas, the next port of call. They'd also have time to hang out together in Key West, Florida, the last port of call before a couple of full days at sea would return the ship to its home port of Galveston. Then the seven-day cruise would be complete. After the stops in Freeport and Key West, Cameron would be on call up until the disembarkation process.

Gabrielle knew what she wanted, but was it the right thing?

The lifeboat session had gone surprisingly well, and Gabrielle had managed to remain calm and professional around Cameron. Pleased with how well she'd handled it, Gabrielle hurried back to her cabin to get ready for her land excursion. She had decided at the last minute that it was okay to allow Cameron to show her around Freeport.

Rushing inside the cabin, she went straight to the bathroom. When she came out, she was wearing a red-and-white polka-dot bikini and a loose, white, gauzy cover-up.

Next she briskly brushed her hair into a ponytail and tied it with a matching polka-dot wrap. Then she began packing her oversize red straw satchel with items she'd need to enjoy a sun-filled day in Freeport. She smiled to herself when she realized that the only thing she'd really need to enjoy the day was Cameron's company.

Cameron anxiously waited for Gabrielle on the ship where a tender would transport them to the island of

Freeport. His eyes scanned the area for any sign of her, hoping she'd make it before the last tender departed. The instant he spotted her a huge grin appeared on his face. "Over here, Gabrielle," he shouted, waving his hands back and forth.

With limited time, Cameron had decided to hire taxis to get around the island. As much as he would have loved to have Gabrielle's arms wrapped around him on a scooter, it wasn't practical.

As soon as they reached the island, Cameron hailed a taxi to Xanadu Beach. With its incredibly beautiful white sand and shallow greenish-blue waters, the beach was unrivaled. Cameron most appreciated that nobody there hassled tourists to buy trinkets and souvenirs. Beaches just didn't come any better than Xanadu.

Gabrielle and Cameron raced across the sand to see who'd be first in the water. This time around she lost. Not only was he way ahead of her, he was already swimming farther out. Once she hit the water, she savored its welcoming warmth. The vivid turquoise water was just as clean as it was at Cable Beach.

Diving underwater, her eyes took in the beauty of fair-size, brightly colored fish. A school of smaller white fish was so close she could scoop them up in her hand. She came up for air, only to go under again a few seconds later. Wondering if she could see more sea life farther out, she began swimming toward the area she'd last seen Cameron in. The water turned frothy from her powerful leg kicks and her steady arm strokes.

Gabrielle resurfaced and looked around for Cameron. He was nowhere in sight, but she felt confident that he was okay, just like he had been at Cable Beach. Moving toward shallower water, she turned over on her back and floated. Once she reached the shoreline, she came out of the water, looked for Cameron and saw that he was already out of the water.

She ran all the way to where they'd left their things, quickly grabbed her beach towel and began drying off. "You sure were in and out of the water in a hurry. Did you even enjoy your dip?"

Cameron chuckled. "Every second of it. How about you?"

"Loved it. Wish we had more time." She appeared thoughtful. "I can't understand why the Gulf of Mexico waters surrounding Galveston Island beaches are so brown when the Caribbean's water is clear as glass. The beaches are also much cleaner."

"It's all about what's on the surface of the water, like seaweed, silt, et cetera. Some water becomes muddy and murky after big storms and hurricanes. Not to mention, beach maintenance is a must in these parts since tourism is the main moneymaking attraction."

After pulling on regular clothes over their swim attire, the couple hastily made their way out onto the bustling streets. Cameron immediately hailed a cab to Lucaya National Park, which was a full-day excursion in itself. Because time was at a premium, they'd explore the park for approximately forty-five minutes before taking another cab to Count Basie Square.

There, Gabrielle and Cameron joined a crowd of locals and tourists dancing in the streets to funky calypso music. It seemed like everyone was having a good time. She danced shoeless with Cameron, and they laughed together and whiled away the short time they had to spend there.

Freeport, she'd heard, had great nightlife; the Joker's

Wild was cited as one of the best club venues. But they wouldn't be able to visit any clubs because the ship would set sail long before sunset. Shopping was another of the island's most popular tourist attractions. At the Straw Market, on Cameron's recommendation, Gabrielle purchased guava jellies for her family and picked up a few things for her own use.

At the International Bazaar, they eyed the indescribable emeralds and other magnificent jewels. Then they went their separate ways to do some clothes shopping for themselves.

Gabrielle wandered into the area of women's island-style clothing. It didn't take her long to see something she liked. She pulled it on in the dressing room, then stepped out and went to the mirror she'd spotted earlier.

As she twirled around and around, she looked at how the soft purple dress looked from the front, sides and back. It was a perfect fit, and she thought it would go nicely with her white sandals. After turning back to the front, she suddenly saw Cameron's image in the mirror. He was right behind her.

Cameron grinned. "Nice dress, lovely color. You should buy it."

Her heart rate was going crazy on her. "I think I will. Thanks for your input." She gave him a sweet smile, then hurried away and disappeared into the dressing room.

Frustrated with the way she made his insides shake like Jell-O, Cameron sighed deeply. A few minutes ago he had been happy about his bargain purchases, but the wind had been knocked out of his sails. He'd never met a woman like Gabrielle, a true designer's original.

To distract himself from his troubling thoughts, he looked down at his watch. He knew full well it was close to the time for grabbing a cab and heading back to the place where they'd catch a tender back to the ship. It wouldn't do for either doctor to get left behind. Missing the boat, literally, would more than likely get them fired.

He walked over to the dressing room. "Gabrielle," he called out softly, "we've got to get going within the next few minutes. It's later than I thought."

Already redressed, she instantly came out of the dressing room. "Do I have time to purchase the dress or should I just forget about it?"

He looked around for an open register. "There," he pointed out to her, "there's no one in line. We have time if you hurry."

"Okay. I'll pay cash." She took off running.

Outside on the street, Cameron hailed the first cab that came by. Once the vehicle stopped, he opened the door and let Gabrielle precede him into the backseat. He slid in right behind her then gave their destination to the driver.

As the cab pulled off, Gabrielle scooted to the other side of the backseat so she could look out the window.

"Scared of being too close to me?" he asked in a teasing tone.

She slowly turned her head to face him. "Want to repeat that?" She'd heard every word he'd said, but she wanted to hear it again.

"No I don't."

Not surprised that he hadn't repeated himself, Gabrielle scooted over the seat until she was right up under him. "Still think I'm scared of closeness?"

He grinned wickedly. "You're a little tease, aren't

you? I think you carry around a lot of fear, but your boldness also surprises me. I like daring. Don't hide it away."

She winked and flashed a flirtatious smile. "There are so many things you have yet to discover. Daring is only a fraction of my personality."

As Cameron slipped between the sheets, he thought of how well the excursion had turned out, though he hadn't expected anything different. He was pleased that he and Gabrielle had more in common than just the same profession, and he liked how easy she was to talk to. Although he had been surprised when Marjorie had asked him to join the dinner party the night before, he had to admit he was excited about it. This situation was a no-win for both him and Gabrielle, yet he still wished things could work out in their favor.

"Love and labor" was how Gabrielle had referred to coworkers dating. He'd never heard that phrase before, but he thought it was rather catchy. He knew scores of people who had loved and labored together, and it hadn't affected them adversely. Husbands and wives both working as doctors wasn't anything out of the ordinary in the world of medicine. He also knew a lot of lawyers married to lawyers, and most of the couples he was well acquainted with were still married.

The big problem for him and her was they'd both been badly burned by mixing work and play. There had to be a way to figure this out. How was it that other couples in the same profession could make it together, yet he and Gabrielle seemed doomed to fail? He was positive there'd been failures among other professionals, but he was only concerned with himself and Gabrielle.

These same questions kept coming to his mind, and Cameron already had the answer as to why it kept on happening. His deep attraction to the woman he worked with was the only possible answer. The gorgeous doctor simply mesmerized him—and he didn't think his attraction to her was going away anytime soon. The playfulness Gabrielle had turned on in the cab had him wanting more of the same. He'd loved her daring and wanted to see how daring she could really be.

Three passengers were waiting at the front door of the clinic when Gabrielle arrived for work. "Hello," she said cheerfully. "Does everyone need to see a doctor?"

The two men and one woman gave positive responses.

Gabrielle smiled. "In that case, I'd better get this door open in a hurry so I can take care of you."

Once Gabrielle was inside, she had the passengers take a seat in the chairs lined against the wall. "I'm Dr. Grinage. I'll be taking care of you. Who was here first?"

One of the men was pointed out by the other two arrivals.

Gabrielle went behind the nurses' station and retrieved the paperwork for patient registration. "Sign in on this sheet," she told them before going back to her office.

She reappeared in seconds, smiling. "Since we're all through with the registration process, let's get started."

The first patient sat still as Gabrielle took his vital signs. Once she had his readings, she escorted him into one of the treatment rooms so they could have privacy. Instead of sitting on the treatment table, the man sat down in a chair. "I'm having muscle spasms in my legs. I didn't think to bring anything to help out."

Hearing the front door open, Gabrielle looked out and saw Cameron come in. She was glad to see she had help, even though she knew she could've effectively handled all three patients.

Smiling, Cameron kicked back with his feet up on his desk. He and Gabrielle had worked so well together the entire shift. There weren't many patients who'd come through all day, but they had expeditiously and thoroughly helped the ones who had.

Gabrielle suddenly popped into Cameron's office. "What're you smiling about?"

"Are you sure you want to know?

"Hmm, it's that bad, huh?"

"It all depends on how you look at it," he responded softly.

She plopped down on a chair. "I have a pretty open mind. Try me, Dr. Quinn."

Before she'd come into the office, Cameron was sure he'd gotten up the nerve to invite Gabrielle to be his guest at the formal dinner sitting less than three hours away. His visions of her in an evening gown had been enough to spur him on.

As he looked her right in the eyes, his hands began to sweat. He took a second to regroup. "Since we've become friends, my question isn't a bad thing. I'd like you to accompany me to the formal dinner this evening."

Gabrielle did her best to hide her shocked reaction. "Of course, I'd love to."

He was surprised that she had accepted, but even more than that, he was extremely pleased.

* * *

The image staring back at Gabrielle in the looking glass was both sophisticated and stunning. The gold lamé formal gown she wore had a low neckline in the front and a cowl neckline that draped dangerously low in the back. A side split added even more sex appeal to her already head-turning look.

Pleased with her appearance, Gabrielle smiled at her reflection, marveling at what she'd accomplished in such a short time. She and Cameron had gotten caught up in a lot of paperwork at the clinic, and she'd made it back to her cabin with not much time to get ready for dinner.

This was Gabrielle's first appearance at a formal night aboard the ship, although one formal had already been held. She had decided not to attend, even though Marjorie had insisted. She had later regretted her decision, but now she could make up for it.

Gabrielle always tried to move forward with her life in general, yet there was a major area in her personal life that was stuck like glue. Wavering over the issue of a romantic liaison and working under Cameron's command kept her frustrated.

This time was different from all the others. Cameron asking her to attend dinner as his companion had made her happy, but then the nagging questions had begun. Getting him out of her mind proved impossible at every attempt.

Marjorie and Tristan would also share Cameron's table, at his request. She admitted to having mixed feelings over them not dining alone, but she was ever mindful that he'd asked her out as his friend. Being asked out as his friend pleased and saddened her, all at the same time. She wanted more than his friendship, yet she was confused and continued to hold back.

Gabrielle jumped suddenly when the phone rang. She peeked at the clock, hoping it wasn't an emergency call or perhaps Cameron calling to cancel. Then a sharp rap came on the door, which sent her into a bit of a tizzy. It was then that she realized how badly her nerves were frayed over her relationship with Cameron.

Gabrielle picked up the phone and carried it to the door. Without peering through the security screen, she swung the door back, only realizing how foolish a move she'd made once she'd put herself at risk. While there was plenty of security aboard the ship, a problem with crime had been mentioned repeatedly in orientation. For more than one reason, she was glad to see Cameron standing there.

"I called first then decided to just pop on over here to see if you're ready to go," Cameron explained.

Gabrielle stared at Cameron as if she was seeing him for the first time. His formal dress was a white jacket and black tuxedo pants. The shoulders were embellished with gold braiding and medical insignias. As blood rushed to her head, Gabrielle felt slightly dizzy. The man was drop-dead gorgeous, and she considered herself superlucky to be his guest for the night. But she also thought Cameron should consider himself just as lucky.

She struggled to locate her voice. "Can you…give me…a minute…to put the phone…back?"

Cameron grinned. "Please promise me you won't run away at midnight."

His sweet remark charmed her. "I promise. I'm yours until—"

He raised both eyebrows. "You'd better be careful there. If I hold you to that, you won't leave my sight. I hope I can hold out another minute."

Gabrielle smiled before going back inside. Cameron was the sweetest man she'd ever come across and his charm was driving her insane.

So was Jordan, in the beginning. No, don't you dare compare Cameron with the likes of him.

Angry with herself for making the comparison, she vowed to never compare Cameron with another man. The gorgeous Dr. Quinn was in a class of his own. She had a hard time believing he'd lead someone on just to break her heart later. Some men were after one thing only—and their game was over once they got it. If she and Cameron turned out to be incompatible, that was one thing, but she was almost sure he'd never purposely wound another human being.

As Gabrielle walked away, Cameron couldn't draw his eyes from her. She looked like a fairy-tale princess and he was ecstatic, wishing there were an easy way to become her Prince Charming. He'd never been more excited about an evening out. Normally Cameron wouldn't bother with the ship's festivities unless it was a special occasion for one of his staffers, but a lot of things had changed since Gabrielle arrived.

She returned, her smile angelic. "It looks like I needed less than a minute."

Cameron turned on the boyish charm. "How'd you know I was missing you?"

"Your spirit summoned me."

Her smile accelerated his heartbeat. "In that case, I'll have to thank my spirit."

Do you have more of the beautiful lipstick you're wearing? Because I want to kiss you hello so badly. Not sure I can wait to kiss you good-night.

He nervously cracked his knuckles. Cameron wasn't sure he should even try any type of romantic move on her. She had no idea he had a hot and heavy craving for her. He glanced at his watch. "We should go now."

Gabrielle stepped out of the cabin. "I'm ready."

She had to be supercareful to conceal how elated she felt to be his date. If he knew how much she wanted to feel his sexy mouth on hers, it would probably have stunned him good.

She knew a romantic liaison wasn't an ideal situation for them, but she still hadn't found a surefire way of curbing the hot desire burning deep inside her. Just being in Cameron's presence had Gabrielle hotter than the desert in summer. Not only did she burn for him, but thoughts of him came to her when she was in bed every night. She yearned for him no matter where she was.

With her arm looped through Cameron's, Gabrielle walked the corridors, loving the thrill of him beside her. So much had changed between them even though neither had uttered a word about how they felt, and it was certainly inappropriate for her to bring it up. Yet he wouldn't look at her that way if he didn't feel something. He seemed attracted to her because he stared at her often, but she'd have to hear it directly from his mouth for confirmation. Gabrielle couldn't help feeling that her and Cameron were sailing on the same waves.

Will those waves ever crest into full-blown passion?

* * *

Seconds after arriving at the Paris dining room, Gabrielle and Cameron cheerfully greeted Marjorie and Tristan. Both women hugged and the guys exchanged firm handshakes. The two couples were then ushered to their reserved table.

Gabrielle smiled at Marjorie. "You look so elegant. Who's your dress designer?"

Marjorie smoothed her hands down over her electric-blue, form-fitting gown. "It's Dior."

Cameron let Gabrielle precede him into the roomy booth. Tristan and Marjorie sat directly across the table from them. Cameron ordered wine for the foursome then they settled down to chat.

"Our next trip is to the Western Caribbean," Cameron mentioned. "We're at sea for two days before we make port in Montego Bay, Jamaica."

"Then move on to the Cayman Islands, right? I think Cozumel is one of our last ports of call," Tristan said. "I love that the *Parisian Paradise* has alternate itineraries." His gaze settled on Gabrielle. "How are you feeling about your first days on sea duty?"

Gabrielle smiled thoughtfully. "It's been interesting. I haven't had any difficulties with my work, and I love meeting people."

Although I am having difficulty trying hard not to fall madly in love with the ship's gorgeous medical commander.

The wine was delivered and poured.

Cameron lifted his glass in a toast. "A toast to each of us. I'd also like to propose a toast to Gabrielle on adjusting to sea life so quickly. Rarely does anyone find it easy, but you seem just fine with it. Cheers."

Everyone touched their glasses together.

At Cameron's suggestion, he and Gabrielle perused one menu together.

Gabrielle looked over at Cameron and smiled. "I think I'll go with the much lighter halibut. I'm sure it will be scrumptious."

Cameron nodded. "I think I'll have something light too." He looked at the other couple. "Have you guys chosen your meals yet?"

Tristan nodded. "We have. If you two are ready to order, I'll call the waiter."

Cameron gestured for him to be his guest.

Thirty minutes had passed by the time the two couples had finished the last course of the meal then desserts, and everyone appeared full and satisfied. Now it was time to walk off a few of those extra calories.

Cameron stood and held out his hand to Gabrielle, helping her out of the booth.

She smiled softly. "I could use a little exercise." She looked down at her watch. "The show won't start for thirty or forty minutes. Do you guys want to walk with us?"

"We're going to hit the casino for a few minutes," Tristan answered. "Save us a seat."

"You got it," Cameron assured. "See you in the theater."

"Good luck at the casino," Gabrielle said. "See you soon."

Cameron took Gabrielle by the hand and they strolled toward the exit. The admiring eyes watching Cameron and Gabrielle weren't lost on him. Diners and crewmembers gave them knowing smiles, no doubt thinking they were an item. No one, not even them, really knew what was between them, but he wished the distance between them would disappear. His deep affection for her was continuing to grow.

Five minutes outside the door, the ship's photographer tried to entice them to pose for him.

"It's up to the lady. What do you think, Gabrielle?"

"I'd love to have my picture taken with you. Are you okay with it?"

Cameron's response was to put his hand lightly on her back and guide her toward the beautiful beach setting the photographer was using as a backdrop.

Gabrielle felt the heat on her bare back from Cameron's hand. With him so close to her she could feel his breath. As his fingers drew circles on her back with the tips of his nails, the heat intensified, making her wish they were off alone, somewhere very private.

The photographer was animated as he placed their hands and heads together. "You two are an amazing-looking pair."

Close enough to kiss Cameron full on the mouth, she took a deep breath. Instead of acting on her strong desire, Gabrielle used her imagination to execute the kiss.

Moving back to his mark, the photographer flashed away with his camera, giving them instructions throughout the shoot. "On this last shot, sir, please look down into her eyes. And miss, please tilt your chin upward and look up at him as if he's the only man in the world for you. That's it. Beautiful! Smile like you just hit a big jackpot in the casino."

Their widened eyes locked together in an intense gaze, a private language all their own.

The flaming fire in Gabrielle's eyes had Cameron nearly hypnotized. Losing himself in their liquid beauty made him want to succumb to her every desire. He was so close to her face that he could actually see flecks of gold coloring in her eyes. The Gabrielle he'd come to know was an intelligent, compassionate, beautiful woman, with lovely eyes, a fabulous figure and the sweetest demeanor and engaging personality. Everything about her said she was a passionate woman, and he wanted to feel her brand of passion up close and personal.

The photographer stopped snapping photos, which jarred them out of their intense connection.

"Wow! This is one of the most natural photos I've taken this evening. You make a stunning pair. Be sure to look for your photos in the art gallery—they won't be hard to find."

Cameron and Gabrielle thanked the photographer and stepped into the near empty theater.

"Where do you want to sit?"

Gabrielle smiled gently. "I like being down front where I can get a really good look at the details in the beautiful and colorful costume designs. When I was a teenager, I wanted to be a fashion designer."

Cameron grinned. "Well, you sure dress the part. I love what you're wearing, and I've admired other outfits you've worn. People constantly check you out. It makes me proud to have you as my date."

Gabrielle smiled, but she had suddenly lost interest in the theater. "Would you be disappointed if we didn't do the theater? I want to be free."

Cameron's eyebrows shot up. "Free? What do you mean by free?" He hoped she didn't want to be free from him. That would make him none too happy.

"Instead of sitting in this theater for the next two

hours, I'd like to continue our stroll around the ship. If we see something that catches our fantasy, we can do that. What do you think? I'll send Marjorie a text about the change in plans."

He smiled, reaching for her hand. "I actually like spontaneity. Let's get out of here!"

Gabrielle always experienced a warm jolt of excitement when her hand was in his. The couple slowly walked the ship and she felt so at ease with him.

As Gabrielle and Cameron came on the main deck, the calypso music, loud and funky, beckoned her. They took a couple more steps then she stopped and began dancing. She came out of her shoes and tossed them aside. Feeling the music flowing through her like liquid fire put her on a natural high, and the wild movements of her body caused her hair to fly like it was riding the tail of a kite.

Gabrielle summoned Cameron with one hand. "Come on. How can you not feel this rhythm?"

Cameron watched her tantalizing hip action for a couple of seconds more before he stripped off his shoes and socks, kicking them toward hers. His jacket came off a few seconds later then he undid a few buttons on his dress shirt. Pulling her toward him, he drew her close enough for their foreheads to touch. In the next second he twirled her away from him and spun her around and around. Their laughter rang out as they kept up with the fast pace of the music. Gabrielle circled him, shaking her hips like a hula dancer. She felt freer than ever before.

Chapter 6

Nearly two hours later Gabrielle still felt energized. She and Cameron had met back up with Marjorie and Tristan on the main deck just as their evening was winding down.

Work was only several hours away for Gabrielle. No sooner would she get to sleep than the alarm clock would sound and send her off and running. However, she wouldn't have given up this night for anything. The entire evening had been perfect so far, and her handsome date had had a huge hand in it. Cameron was as sincere and sweet as he was good-looking.

Outside in the corridor, Marjorie pulled Gabrielle aside. "Tristan and I are going to the late-night buffet. Do you want to go? I'm asking you separately to keep from putting either of you on the spot."

Gabrielle shook her head. "I'm sorry, but all the vigorous activity has me nearing burnout, and my shoes probably won't fit my swollen feet. I feel great, but I don't want to get worn down completely." Turning down the offer made Gabrielle feel bad, but she had to do what was best for her. Duty came first.

Marjorie briefly took her hand. "Not a problem. We'll have plenty of evenings to hang out. Tristan and I won't be out too much longer."

Marjorie was also on duty tomorrow, so Gabrielle figured she probably had firsthand knowledge of how she felt. As the two women went their separate ways, they said good-night.

Surprising Gabrielle, Cameron picked her up and carried her over to one of the deck chairs. He had retrieved her shoes. As his eyes deeply connected with hers, he slipped each shoe in place. "I can't tell you how many trips I've sailed as the ship's medical commander, but none has been this fun and exciting. I will carry the memory of this one until I'm too old to remember, and until then, I'm looking forward to recalling every minute. Thanks for bringing me stiff shots of wild and crazy thrills."

Gabrielle was speechless and slightly teary over how he'd bared his emotions. Her emotional state had to respond for her—and she hoped he knew the tears were happy ones. Cameron walked Gabrielle home. At the door, Cameron had to fight hard to hold back his desire to taste her inviting mouth. "Thanks for coming out with me. I really enjoyed your company." Staring into her eyes was almost more than he could bear.

Gabrielle gently put her hand on Cameron's arm. "Thanks for asking me out. And you're welcome. This evening was fantastic from beginning to end. I hope you never forget one moment of any of the time we've shared. I know I won't. See you in the morning."

"I wish this night didn't have to end. But all good things must come to an end, or so they say."

"I'm not sure I agree. I know all about endings. We're only ending the evening, but we're just beginning to build something fantastic between us, Cameron." She shrugged. "I don't know, but it seems like we have no control over what's taken on a life of its own."

Cameron smiled broadly. "I love losing control in this instance. Only you could have been the one to put the fun and joy back in my intense life. On that note, I'll say good-night." His eyes showed his desire to spend the rest of the night holding Gabrielle in his arms.

On tiptoes, Gabrielle pressed her lips against his right cheek then left, wishing she had the nerve to kiss his mouth instead. *Friends now, but soon to be lovers* clicked inside her head. Without further thought, she slipped her key card into the slot and went inside.

Cameron stood in the hallway for several seconds before he moved next door.

Finished hanging up her formal attire, Gabrielle slipped on a black lacy nightgown. The sexy gown was perfect for the waves of desire she was experiencing. The simple kisses to Cameron's cheeks had left her physically aroused. She felt incredibly sexy and desirable every time she was with him, and these wonderful feelings hadn't happened to her in a long while.

As she lay on the bed, she looked up at the ceiling and watched the fan go round and round. The slight whirring of the blades was hypnotic and lulled her into a peaceful state. It was hard to believe she felt this serene when her emotions were still getting roughed up pretty darn good. Her heart yearned madly for the man next door. The same man she should consider only her friend was much more than that to her. And that same man was also her boss. His attentiveness when he had slipped on her shoes had blown her mind.

Tears slipped from her eyes. Coming aboard this ship might've been a huge mistake. Keeping herself from mixing love and labor was getting harder and harder by the second. She had to work with Cameron, but staying away from him after work hours would be painful and difficult. How could she ignore her feelings for the very person who'd led her back to hope and passion?

Gabrielle hated the situation she found herself in, but she was not a quitter. Leaving the job was not an option. She would stay on until the end of her commitment, and her love for everything about the job would keep her strong. She saw how cruising could become addictive, but much more than cruising had her strung out. She was highly addicted to Commander Quinn.

Early the next morning, dressed only in undergarments, Gabrielle rushed out of the bathroom and picked up the phone. "Hello, Gabrielle here."

"Good morning." It was Marjorie. "I know I'll see you in the clinic, but the last couple of days before disembarkation can get crazy. There's a private party tonight, and I'd like you to come."

"Where and when?" Gabrielle asked.

"It hasn't been finalized, but I'll let you know before the end of the day. Is that okay?"

"It is, but I'll only be able to go for a short while.

There are some personal things I'd like to do before we disembark and set sail for the new itinerary."

"Not a problem. I'll see you in the clinic."

Gabrielle hung up the phone. After returning to the bathroom to finish getting ready for work, she thought about the party. She wasn't much of a partygoer, but she had promised to open herself up to all sorts of new things since the first day of the cruise. She didn't want to seem standoffish, and mingling with her coworkers would be a blast. It was the same way in private practice. The majority of the folks she hung out with were just like her: medical professionals.

Finished with brushing her teeth and applying moisturizer to her face, Gabrielle left the bathroom and went into the alcove, where she put on makeup and sprayed on a light perfume. After slipping on her starched white uniform, she took a last glance in the mirror.

She was now prepared for work, both mentally and physically.

By the time Gabrielle got to the clinic, the other staff members were present and accounted for. Even Joseph was there, which meant he'd gotten there ahead of the scheduled time.

Gabrielle's forehead creased with worry when she realized that the large group of patients was crewmembers. Had something bad happened? Perhaps they were there to get checked out before the ship sailed its next itinerary. It could be standard practice. If it was, she hadn't read about it in the manual, nor had anyone mentioned it. She sighed, knowing she'd find out shortly. They were in Key West, which was the last stop. The ship wouldn't be in port for long before heading back to sea for the trip back home.

Cameron rapidly came down the hallway and turned the corner. Just as Gabrielle turned the same corner, the two doctors collided.

As he reached out to keep her from falling, his tenderness caused her heart to race. The scent of his cologne brushed by her nose, and she inhaled it as if it was a part of him.

Once Gabrielle was on solid footing, Cameron released his hold on her, wishing he didn't have to. "Good morning. It's great to see you. How'd you sleep last night?"

Gabrielle chuckled. "I had to be in a deep one. It was the first time I didn't wake up in the wee hours of the morning. I think I'm getting used to my new home." *The way I desperately want to get used to you being at my side.*

"Glad to hear it." Slipping his hand under her elbow, he guided her down the hallway then directed her into his office and shut the door. He appeared somewhat disturbed. "We may have a real problem on our hands. I'm sure you saw the number of male crewmembers waiting to be seen."

Gabrielle put her hand under her chin. "How could I not see? What's up?"

"The two crewmembers I've spoken with have flu-like symptoms, but it could also be an outbreak of something more serious. I'm waiting on blood results."

Gabrielle's eyes widened. "Something that's highly contagious?"

Cameron shrugged. "It's possible, but I wouldn't say that to anyone but you until I had proof of it. It's not terribly unusual for a foreign or domestic crewmember to bring TB on board. It always amazes me when it happens. The strict pre-employment physical includes lab work, X-rays and checking and updating inoculations. It's no joke. But it stumps me how those infected manage to slide by. We've already picked up new crewmembers for the return home."

Gabrielle swiped her hand across her forehead. "I know we don't want to spread panic, not without just cause. I hope it's only the flu. It can spread quickly, but it's the lesser of two evils. What should we do in the meantime?"

He faced her and firmly placed his hands on her arms. "I don't want you to do anything. Go into your office and stay there until I call you. We have to stay protected, but I don't want to resort to masks and sterile cover-ups and alarm everyone."

Gabrielle's eyes thundered. "Please don't ask me to do that. I'm a doctor, and I've taken the same oath as you. My place is with anyone who comes in for help. I'll be up front in a minute." Without waiting for Cameron to comment, she turned and walked away.

Cameron stared after her. He was annoyed at her but not angry. He respected her and the position she'd taken. She was right—her allegiance was to the patient. Asking her to hide away in an office had been worse than insensitive. Cameron made a quiet promise to apologize before day's end.

Although Gabrielle was offended by Cameron's command, she wouldn't let it interfere with her duty or their relationship. She had handled it the right way and had firmly stood her ground. As far as she was concerned, it was over and done with. She put her things away, slipped on a lab coat, and headed straight for the front nurses' station.

Her smile was as bright as a sunny day as she swung into the reception area. There was plenty of pep in her step, and her engine was revved up and ready to handle overdrive.

The nurses had already taken vital signs of all the patients, including some new ones who'd showed up. Gabrielle checked the sign-in sheet and called the name of the next person. A young guy got to his feet.

Gabrielle quickly ushered him into a treatment cubicle and onto the padded table. "Want to tell me your symptoms?"

"I had a fever last night, but it's even higher this morning. One minute I'm hot then I get cold chills."

Gabrielle looked up from writing in the medical record. "Do you have any coughing, runny nose, nausea, vomiting or sore throat?"

"Dinner didn't stay down last evening, but my chest is what I'm worried about. It's tight and it's hard for me to breathe at times. Every muscle is aching."

Gabrielle added more notes to the chart. "Your temperature *is* elevated. Blood pressure is fine. With your permission, we want to draw your blood for testing. Is that okay?"

"Yes, ma'am, it is. We can't report back to duty until we're treated. I don't know if it's been mentioned or not, but all of us crewmembers are assigned to the same dorm."

"Thank you. That's helpful. Relax and give me a few minutes to get everything set up."

"None of us are in a hurry, Dr. Grinage. We just want to know what's happening."

Cameron had called a brief staff meeting in the small conference room. Once everyone was seated, he stood.

"Good morning, crew. Thanks for attending." He laughed. "As if you had a choice! No, none of us had a choice. What we have is an emergency to deal with. We have to continue pulling together to get our crewmembers taken care of. You're doing great with the patients and all medical procedures, and I appreciate each of you. Dr. Grinage has something to say, which is the main reason we're meeting." Cameron presented Gabrielle then took a seat.

"Good morning. I'm glad you're here today. What I heard from one of the crewmembers may shed some light on this medical dilemma. All the crewmembers out there are from the same dorm. There may be contamination and possibly cross-contamination. It may be as simple as a cold or flu passing among them. It could be something much worse. We already know it's contagious. Without running lab tests, no one can be certain of what needs to be dealt with. We may have to go the whole nine yards on this one, guys. Thanks for your attention." She yielded the floor back to Cameron.

"Thank you, Dr. Grinage. Knowing they're all from the same dorm is important information. However, crewmembers mingle, and many of them work in food preparation. Blood and urine tests will have to be given to every crewmember and anyone else who comes in with the same symptoms."

Cameron explained that one part of the clinic was closed off to everyone but the members of the crew that lived in the same dorm. The passengers would be seen in the front treatment rooms, along with crewmembers from other dorms who didn't exhibit the same symptoms. He told his staff that he'd fill out a number of lab slips indicating blood and urine samples and that all specimens should be brought to him for immediate testing.

"Before drawing blood or taking urine, make sure the crewmember's name and dorm number is on the lab forms, blood vials and urine cups. We're a team, one of the best medical teams in the fleet. Let's get out there and do what we do best."

The staff moved into the middle of the room then joined hands. As hands broke free, they raised their arms high and shouted out a cheer. It was a show of solidarity.

Gabrielle and Cameron stood back and watched the departure of the medical staff.

Cameron smiled. "We have a dedicated team. You'll see their greatness over time."

"I've already seen it over and over. They work well together and they're not hung up on titles or who's in charge. Both the men and women aren't afraid to jump into a problem without knowing what they're dealing with."

Cameron nodded. "Great assessment, Gabrielle. I couldn't have said it better myself."

Gabrielle was seated on the sofa, thinking about the clinic's business of the day. Both shifts at the infirmary had become overrun with crewmembers from the same dorm. Everyone had missed lunch and not one person had taken issue with it. The situation had called for undivided attention, and that was exactly how the crew had gone about doing their jobs.

All blood tests and urine samples had come back negative. X-rays had been negative for TB. White counts were elevated, pointing to signs of infection. They had identified specific bacteria that proved influenza was more than likely the cause. No quarantines had been warranted, and antibiotics had been given to manage the infection.

Each crewmember was scheduled to return to the clinic for a recheck before the next embarkation in Galveston. The first hours in home port would keep the clinic staff very busy, because everyone had to be medically cleared for each sailing.

Gabrielle knew the next few days would be hectic, but for now she had to get ready for Marjorie's party. She dressed in slim black pants with a wide belt and a lovely white top and looked into the mirror to make sure her apparel was appropriate for a party. Marjorie had informed her that a private party would be held in a reserved section of the main club, Paris after Dark.

There weren't a huge number of medical staff members, but she thought they'd have a good time. She got along well with the nurses and she and Cameron got along only too well.

As Gabrielle turned the corner to reach the clinic's reserved section in the club, she was surprised by a burst of noise and cheering from her coworkers. They yelled "Congratulations on your first cruise" in unison. Lightbulbs flashed, loud clapping thundered, and wolf whistles and boisterous cheering rang out.

Gabrielle was stunned. As her eyes adjusted to the flashing lights and brightly lit disco ball, she saw a sparkling banner with her name emblazoned in gold lettering. Her hand went up to her heart and tears came to her eyes. Marjorie hadn't said the party was for her—and she was totally bowled over by it.

Dressed in black dress slacks and a lightweight white sweater, Cameron came out to meet Gabrielle. As they came face-to-face, he extended his arm to her. "Let me escort you back to our table. You really looked surprised—and you are stunning. I'm glad this party was kept under wraps, since the majority of our surprise events get leaked."

As Gabrielle took Cameron's arm, she looked him over. She laughed when she saw that they wore the same colors. It was as if they had planned it.

Gabrielle suddenly felt a burst of energy. Her eyes grew wide from the excitement of the moment. "This is unreal. Do all new employees get a party? It's hard to express myself right now, I feel so honored."

"You're the main focus, but we do include new clinic crewmembers in our surprise gatherings. Their banner is hung a little farther back. You'll see it when you get closer."

"Who planned this?" Gabrielle asked.

"Marjorie and I put our heads together, because you're special and we wanted to convey our feelings and appreciation. We're especially proud of how you've handled your first week. Every new clinic crewmember has had one thing or another to complain about, but not you. We haven't heard you make a single disgruntled remark. That in itself is remarkable."

Full of emotion, Gabrielle shook her head. "Why am I not surprised that Marjorie was involved? I'm so moved by the wonderful gesture, Cameron. But I'm only doing the job I was hired to do. I truly appreciate the recognition, and it means a lot to me."

"I can see how much it means to you." Cameron gently squeezed her hand.

Once they'd reached the back of the room, the staff swarmed Gabrielle. Many reached out to give her a warm hug. She couldn't stop the tears from streaking down her face. Her coworkers had gone to great lengths to honor her and the new nurses.

Gabrielle received warm greetings from two clinic doctors she hadn't worked with but had met during staff meetings. Both men were tall, very handsome, and had supersweet personalities. They were also both single and eligible.

Dr. Phillip Sumner and Dr. Patrick Patterson were every bit as dedicated to the medical profession as she and Cameron. She was scheduled to work with each physician on the next itinerary, and Gabrielle was thrilled about the upcoming sailing, which included Jamaica.

Once the greetings and warm hugs were out of the way, Cameron led Gabrielle to the reserved table that had a great view of the dance floor. Gabrielle took pleasure in sizing up the glitzy club that promised a great night of music, dancing and fun.

Marjorie and Tristan stood side by side in front of the decorated table. The couple warmly embraced the new friend they'd so easily made in Gabrielle.

Marjorie looked sheepish. "Sorry I duped you, but we really wanted to surprise you."

Gabrielle laughed heartily. "Mission accomplished."

Marjorie and Tristan escorted her to a nearby table, where a beautiful sheet cake iced in yellow and blue

sat on a pedestal. Large letters spelling out congratulations, and Gabrielle's name had been penned on the
cake with blue-and-yellow icing. The full sheet cake
served beautifully as a centerpiece for an array of delicious looking finger foods. Another sheet cake was
decorated with lavender roses and yellow piping, and
the names of the three new nurses were written on it.

"This really is too much," Gabrielle said excitedly.
"The cakes are beautiful. Thank you, guys, so much. I
feel extra special, not duped."

"You are extra special," Marjorie said, giving Gabrielle another hug.

"I second that," Tristan said.

Cameron slipped his arm around Gabrielle. "We have
a third confirmation here. Do you want to sit down or
mingle?"

Gabrielle smiled. "I should mingle. After all, this is
my party, too. The new nurses and I should hang out
together for a while."

"Joanie, Candi and Carolyn will love it. Enjoy yourself, and I'll be right here when you get back," Cameron assured her.

As Gabrielle walked away from the table, she
couldn't stop smiling. Inside she was quivering and
her heart was full. Besides her family, no one had ever
thrown her a surprise party or shown her how much she
was appreciated after only one week. Her coworkers
were extraordinary. If she stayed true to herself, she'd
make many friends aboard the ship.

Cameron's words from his orientation speech echoed
inside her head. *We're all one big happy family.* Her
eyes glistened with moisture. *So true,* she thought. She
missed her family more and more with each passing

day, but she now had a second family to help ease the separation.

Before Gabrielle could begin mingling, Phillip Sumner took her hand and whirled her onto the dance floor. She was surprised, but she couldn't embarrass him or herself by turning back. Yet the last place she wanted to be was on an empty dance floor with a colleague she didn't really know.

It's all in fun. This is a party and I'm one of the honorees. Anything could happen.

The look on Cameron's face wasn't exactly a happy one. As he watched Gabrielle dancing with Phillip, a jealous streak ripped at his heartstrings. Never before had he experienced anything akin to envy. He didn't like the way it made him feel, yet he understood these new feelings. The woman he called his friend was so much more than that to him. She had stolen his heart without any effort on her part.

Rephrase that, pal. You willingly ripped out your heart and donated it to Gabrielle.

The other partygoers clapped, cheered and whistled for the dancing couple. Phillip had some great dance moves, and Gabrielle's were none too shabby. Her slender body rocked and gyrated to the pulsating rhythms of the blaring music, and it wasn't long before she just relaxed and let her hair down.

Gabrielle saw Patrick come onto the dance floor without a partner. When he cut in on Phillip, she blushed from embarrassment. They were the only two people on the dance floor, which meant they were the center of attention. The thought unnerved her, and she hoped Marjorie would rescue her.

Gabrielle changed partners through four fast-paced songs, then all the ladies in the house rushed onto the dance floor and quickly shooed the men away. After pulling together as a group, they began one of the newest line dances. The music was rocking and the women loved it. As though they'd rehearsed the dance together, they stayed in perfect sync while effortlessly executing the complicated dance steps.

Gabrielle was so grateful she already knew the steps. Otherwise, she would've been mortified at looking clumsy until she'd caught on. She didn't even think of leaving the floor, since it was a fun dance, as most line dances were. Like the others, Gabrielle had no problem keeping up.

Songs were constantly spun by the DJ without any noticeable gaps, until a slow song suddenly came through the speakers. Men flocked back to the floor, pairing off with ladies of their choice. Phillip headed straight for Gabrielle, but stiff competition beat him to the punch.

Cameron brought Gabrielle into his arms, holding her close. "You're something else," he whispered into her ear.

"Want to define that statement for me?" she whispered back. As her lips had come into contact with his ear, she felt a strong physical reaction.

"I see that you have skills in quite a few areas," he flirted. "There's much more to you than meets the eye. I wonder what other areas of expertise you haven't unleashed on me yet. You sure know your way around the dance floor, and you possess some serious hip action. Some of the men were practically drooling."

Gabrielle laughed, deciding not to respond to Cameron's last comments. He was the only man in the room she'd love to have drooling over her. As for her hips, they'd shake, rattle and roll for him at any given time.

"Commander, you may never know the vast number of skills I possess. But if you stick around, you might discover more," she said. "Dr. Gabrielle Grinage is not an open book, and to read and understand my autobiography will take endurance and patience. Think you have what it takes?"

As usual, when he was around Gabrielle, Cameron's heart reacted to his ever-growing feelings for her. "The answer is a resounding yes. First off, I'm long on patience. I've been referred to as an offspring of father patience. And your story isn't something I'd have to endure—it'd be my pleasure. I definitely have a strong interest in learning more about the things that fascinate me."

Her eyes blinked a few times. "Wow! I'm going to have to drink that in slowly so I can savor every word."

Gabrielle's heart reacted to Cameron the same way his did. Being this close to him was always pleasurable and agonizing at the same time. That's the way it was when the heart was compromised. Gabrielle realized she had no control whatsoever over the feelings that had taken up residence in her heart. What she felt was strong and undeniable. Serving an eviction notice on her feelings wouldn't do any good, either. Cameron had cut through her pain and had somehow made her feel whole again.

With a cordless microphone in her hand, Marjorie

stood in the center of the dance floor. "I need your attention for just a moment." She turned to see if Tristan had been successful at corralling Gabrielle, Joanie, Candi and Carolyn in one spot. He gave her the thumbs-up sign once he had them all together.

"Thanks to Tristan, we have all our new employees in one place." She called each of the four women by name. "This is our way of honoring you and welcoming you to our special crew. It has been a pleasure working with each of you on this itinerary. Please join me in giving these ladies a heartfelt welcome aboard."

There was thundering applause throughout the club.

Marjorie tapped the microphone, drawing attention back to her. "One more thing before we let you go back and party the night away. Dr. Grinage, can you please come forward for a special presentation? Dr. Quinn, I'll need you, too."

On rickety legs Gabrielle made it up front and stepped to the left of Marjorie. Cameron crossed the room in a hurried manner, and Marjorie handed him something. Cameron accepted four small packages from Marjorie, and took the microphone and walked over to Gabrielle. He gave her a kiss on each cheek, infusing color into her complexion. He then made the same warm gesture to the nurses.

Cameron held up a gold anchor on a sparkling gold chain. "Our entire crew presents these gifts to you for your dedicated service and unwavering professionalism. Your willingness to stick with your crew and to help out through thick and thin has endeared all of you to us. We thank you from the bottom of our hearts!"

Dr. Quinn first circled Gabrielle's neck with a beautiful dainty gold chain holding an engraved 24-karat gold anchor. Loud cheers and heavy rounds of applause filled the club. "The date on the anchors coincides with your first day at sea. Your crew and I stand behind all of you. Good luck!" Cannon hugged Gabrielle then moved on to the nurses.

No sooner had Cameron moved away to reclaim his seat, than the line leading up to the honorees began steadily growing. He wasn't surprised that his entire crew was in line. They had taken to the ladies like bees to honey, and had frequently expressed to him how much they thoroughly enjoyed working with the new ladies.

However, for Cameron, Gabrielle was the biggest hit, but it wasn't as if he hadn't seen this coming. He'd constantly watched her with crewmembers and passengers.

Gabrielle had touched the hearts and souls of many in such a short span of time.

Starting to feel the fizz draining from her fizzle, Gabrielle was ready to turn off the lights on the disco ball. If she danced through one more song, fast or slow, it wouldn't have surprised her if her feet blew up. Her statement about staying at the club only for a short time rang in her ears menacingly. She had lasted a lot longer than she had imagined, but then again, she was an honoree.

Gabrielle scanned the dance floor, hoping to catch up with Marjorie to tell her she was leaving, but Marjorie was nowhere to be seen. She'd just have to explain it to her on duty tomorrow. It seemed to her that the three honored nurses had also left the club, and in fact, there were very few people still in the reserved section.

It took what little strength Gabrielle had left to get to

the nearest exit. To keep from putting her full weight on her feet, she walked gingerly. As she reached one of the exit doors, she closed her eyes momentarily and smiled. No matter how tired she was, this had been a great night—and she'd been honored in such a lovely way.

Chapter 7

The moment Cameron had seen Gabrielle practically dragging herself toward the exit, he began to worry. He wasn't sure if she was sick or just plain tired from the earlier emergency in the clinic. It had been a long day for his staff, and most of the crewmembers had departed, so he decided to leave the club to see Gabrielle home safely.

He quickly caught up to her. "Are you okay?"

Gabrielle smiled weakly. "I've never been this tired in my life. I think today's emergency drained me. I had very little rest between leaving the clinic and coming to the party."

Cameron momentarily slipped his arm around her shoulders. "A good night's sleep should get you back on track. I think all of us are tired since we did have a rough time of it today. Mind me walking you to your cabin? We are neighbors, after all."

"I'd love the company. It gets kind of eerie in the corridors at night."

"I can imagine how that might feel for any woman alone. I've got you covered."

"Thanks, Cameron, I appreciate it."

As they boarded the elevator, his thoughts were solely on her. "I'm happy you had a good time. I could tell it was a total surprise by the way it was etched on your pretty face. Do you like the anchor?"

Gabrielle fingered it. "It's beautiful, much like the one you wear. You were a sailor once so it's more appropriate for you."

"You're a sailor now, Gabrielle, just a civilian sailor. If you don't want the anchor around your neck, put it on a charm bracelet."

Gabrielle smiled. "Great idea!"

Cameron came even closer to her to gently touch the necklace. It felt really good to be so close, his hand so near her breast as he fingered the anchor. She smiled at the thought that he was there with her because he wanted to be. He could've stayed in the club and hung out, but instead he chose to escort her home.

When they reached her cabin fifteen minutes later, she briefly thought about asking him in, then decided it was a better idea not to. As a case of nervousness hit her, she fumbled in her purse for the key card.

She turned to face Cameron. "Lights out," she joked. "I should be in tip top shape tomorrow…or later today actually. Thanks for a lovely night and the great surprise. I had a super time, and everything was so nice. Are you going back to the party?"

Cameron looked right into her eyes. "Do you want me to go back?"

Gabrielle didn't know what to say. His question had thrown her off. "Whether you go back or not isn't up to me."

"Well, no, I'm not interested in going back. Now if you were to ask me in, I'd accept the invite before you released your next breath."

Unsure of herself and Cameron, Gabrielle wished she could give him an answer.

Telling him to go home was rude— and she wasn't sure that was what she really wanted.

Cameron didn't give her much time to think. His urge to taste her mouth had won out over his attempt to cool himself down. Lifting her chin with two fingers, Cameron lowered his head until their lips met. To gauge her reaction, he dusted her lips with several soft kisses. Then his forefinger slowly outlined her mouth.

Looking down into her mesmerizing eyes, Cameron tried to see if he'd moved too fast or been inappropriate. She appeared a bit startled but didn't seem to object to his show of affection. The blush on her cheeks was a telltale sign.

Giving it no more thought, his top lip skirted her bottom one, causing her breath to come in short spurts. She hadn't pushed him away. He took it as a good sign and hoped he wasn't making a mistake. He didn't want to lose her, and he already cared enough for her to risk his heart again.

As his lips teased hers, his heart rate sped up. It felt like a runaway freight train was loose inside his chest. His sex responded to his desire for her, and he wrapped his arms around her tightly, kissing her with deep passion.

The intimate exchange caused his entire body to

ache with longing. His insides quivered and his nerves twanged. His body felt as if it was on fire. Moving his arms from around her, he cupped her face between his hands and kissed her thoroughly. The woman's luscious mouth drove him wild, making him want to kiss her endlessly. The feel of her kissing him back was indescribable. He'd never felt a kiss so completely. Gabrielle had the sweetest kisses; the kind a man didn't mind getting addicted to.

Trembling all over, Gabrielle savored the sweet taste of Cameron's mouth. His kisses had her floating somewhere she'd never been before. The feeling of completion was totally foreign to her. As his tongue sought out hers, she gasped with pleasure and opened herself up to receive it. The thought to back away from him lasted only a second.

Kissing Cameron was much too enjoyable to think of bringing the passion to an abrupt end. Completely surrendering her mouth to his, she felt her body trembling from the sweet sensations, which only made her want more and more of him.

"Maybe we should move inside," he whispered into her ear.

"Yes…probably," she responded mindlessly. With her key card now tucked in her hand, she tried opening the door, but her fingers shook badly.

Taking the card from Gabrielle's hand, Cameron opened the door. Once inside, he kicked the door shut and brought her back into his arms, resuming the intimate assault on her hungrily awaiting mouth. Pressing her back against the door, he closed the minute distance between them, starting a wildfire he couldn't put out the way he wanted to.

They shared several sensuous kisses as her frenzied fingers raked through his hair. The feel of his hair between her fingers was exhilarating to Gabrielle. She loved its thickness. Her breathing became labored, and she struggled to suck in enough air to breathe evenly. Kissing in the darkness of her cabin only fueled the fire even more.

Cameron pulled back to give her time to catch her breath, but he kept his arms around her. "Kissing you is incredible." He shrugged. "And I guess it's too late to ask if I'm out of line."

Gabrielle reached up and smoothed his brows with her thumb. Her stomach somersaulted as she struggled to regain composure. "I have to ask you something. As much as I'm enjoying it, should we be doing this?"

"The same question has run through my head. I've wanted to kiss you since the day I met you. And if you don't want me to kiss you again, it'll be hard to deal with. But your needs and desires come first with me. I'll do what you think is best."

Looking like she was lost somewhere among the clouds, Gabrielle shook her head. "I honestly don't know what's best for me right now. I do know I like how you make me feel. I'm just not big on mixing work and pleasure."

"That's also been the rule of thumb for me. The problem is I can't put my rules into play with you, and I can't imagine my desire for you going away."

"But being badly burned by indulging in a love affair with a coworker can do you in. You know how that feels, too. I really don't know what to do… Maybe we should sleep on it. What do you think?" Gabrielle asked.

"All I can think about right now is how much I enjoyed kissing you. You turn me on and I won't lie about it. We both got burned, but that's our past. And it's not like we haven't already discussed this matter. We both know the score—I'm not Jordan and you're not Amanda."

Cameron drew Gabrielle closer and tenderly kissed her again. Their kisses quickly grew in passion and deeper in intensity, making a scorching heat continue to mount between them. The wild thrills threatened Gabrielle's willpower.

As her common sense began to return, she pulled away. "We'd better get a grip. I can't think clearly with so much passion and heat surrounding me. Maybe we should say good-night before we do something we might regret."

"So, you *do* want me as much as I want you. Well, I'll leave before we commit what might be a cardinal sin." He grinned.

Making love to her was anything but a sin. If he ever got the chance to make love to her, he'd consider it a miracle. "Sleep well. At least I know I'll go to sleep with a smile on my face."

Cameron kissed Gabrielle once again then opened the door and left.

Standing in the doorway, Gabrielle stared after him, hoping he'd look back at her. When he didn't turn around, she closed the door.

Disappointed that she'd brought the burning passion between them to a screeching halt, Gabrielle walked through her cabin and over to her bed, where she plopped down. Her brain felt scrambled and her libido was screaming for release.

A couple of minutes later, Gabrielle stripped down, still terribly confused by what had occurred between her and Cameron. Without bothering to hang up her clothes or put on sleepwear, she climbed into bed. Before she could even close her weary eyes, the phone rang. She held her breath, guessing that the caller was Cameron. She hoped against hope that it was him calling to assure her everything was still okay between them.

It could be an emergency, she thought, even though she knew on-call communications came only through the cell. As she picked up the bedside extension, she sighed then gave a near breathless greeting once she heard Cameron's voice.

"Hope I didn't wake you. It was hard for me to fall asleep without knowing if you're okay. I won't apologize for my actions, but please don't beat yourself up over what happened between us. We'll figure this out. I don't want you to have any regrets. I have none, Gabrielle."

"I don't have any, either, but I have concerns. How do we work together and keep our attraction under wraps? I'm so attracted to you."

"You're not alone in being attracted. I've wanted you from day one. We're both adults, Gabby, and I think we can handle things at work. Let's see what happens before we put our own heads on the chopping block."

"Gabby," she repeated softly. "That's what my family calls me, but I correct anyone else who does it. Coming from you, though, it sounded like a sweet term of endearment, just as it is with my family. I like how it made me feel."

"Does that mean I can use it? I *do* mean it as an endearment."

"It's fine when we're alone, but not in public. I don't want people to get the wrong idea."

"I'm glad I can call you Gabby in private, but what exactly is the wrong idea? That we're attracted to each other and want to get to know each other better?"

"Some of our coworkers might think we're intimately involved. For one, Marjorie already thinks I have a major crush on you."

"I consider a crush different from pure attraction. Is Marjorie correct?"

Gabrielle chuckled softly. "I plead the Fifth. I don't kiss and tell."

Cameron laughed. "Lady, you're something else. I enjoy you so much."

"Same here. It's really late and we have an early wakeup call. Sleep tight, Cameron."

"Thanks. We need to talk about our attraction. And we should do it soon."

"I'm worried I won't be able to stop thinking about it," Gabrielle said breathlessly.

Disappointed that she had ended the call so abruptly, Cameron cradled the receiver, wishing he'd encouraged more conversation. With a perfect image of her popping into his head, he wondered if she slept in the nude. The thought of her lying naked in bed was both appealing and frustrating to him. Sex wasn't first and foremost in his mind, and it wasn't something he ever intended to push on her. Everything between them had to come naturally, and they had to be of one accord. But by

Gabrielle's response, he was sure they had both wanted the ignited passion.

He remembered how Gabrielle had looked in a bathing suit after several hours in the sun had painted her body a deep bronze, which made her even more alluring. Her chestnut hair was enhanced by her tan, and he loved seeing the breeze playing in her hair.

When he'd carried her into the sea earlier in the cruise, he'd had the perfect opportunity to touch parts of her bare flesh, and her firm, shapely figure had been an ideal fit against his muscular body. Kissing her tonight had taken courage.

Cameron was both physically and mentally exhausted. He was too tired to put his brain through the grinder over something he had no control over. Thinking about Gabrielle was always pleasant, but he was afraid they might not happen as a couple. Although she tried to be brave, he'd seen some fear in her eyes. He was somewhat fearful, too, fearful that Gabrielle had been hurt too deeply to try love again.

Ready to clear his mind and fall into a deep sleep, Cameron closed his eyes. For the next half hour, he tossed and turned, unable to stop thinking about Gabrielle, the woman next door.

The *Parisian Paradise* would be at sea less than twenty-four hours before making port back home in Galveston. Gabrielle felt energized, and the thought of seeing her family made her smile. She'd awakened at least an hour before her alarm clock was scheduled to go off, had showered and was now ready to report for duty.

Gabrielle thought of Cameron. What had happened between them was amazing. For a couple of hours she had lain awake, worrying over what havoc a change in their relationship could wreak upon them. It was surprising that she'd finally gotten off to sleep in the wee hours of the morning.

His kisses, the type of passionate kisses she couldn't get enough of, had brought her to her knees. It seemed like forever since their first and last kiss. She still regretted having brought the passion to an end. Her body had been on fire for him, and the heat hadn't lessened one bit since then.

Grabbing a ceramic bowl of steaming oatmeal off the counter, she took it over to the table and sat down to eat. She wasn't hungry, yet she had to eat to maintain strength. They'd sail into Galveston around 7:00 a.m., and she wanted to be energized to see her family. She wanted them to see she'd fared well on the first week of her new job.

Gabrielle expected to see the entire family at the dock around noon, unless one of her brothers had medical emergencies. They only had a few hours to be together, but she would've been happy with any amount of time. She still didn't know if they'd get to come aboard the ship or if she would disembark. It was something she had to arrange through Cameron, and she planned to do that as soon as they both made it to the clinic.

Gabrielle dropped her spoon in the bowl. She suddenly felt emotional, hoping things wouldn't change for her and Cameron because of the passion they'd shared. She felt a lot for him, and she worried that their attraction might interfere with the friendship they'd engaged in so naturally and so comfortably. Losing him as a friend would hurt.

"Losing him as a lover wouldn't be any less painful," Gabrielle pondered aloud.

As coworkers, how could they become lovers? Wasn't the deck stacked a mile high against them? A bright future towered a mile high over them; well, a mile high against them was more like it. It felt awful to want something she couldn't have. But it wasn't just a desire for something. It was a desire for Dr. Cameron Quinn, a man she had fallen fast for.

Gabrielle took a deep breath before walking into the clinic. She wasn't even sure if Cameron was in yet, but her nerves had already taken her over. Squaring her shoulders, she went inside, telling herself that everything would be okay. Both she and Cameron had been willing partners in a passion fest, and neither one could blame the other for what had happened. And it wouldn't matter anyway, because they had thoroughly enjoyed each other.

Leaning against the front counter, Cameron wore a beautiful smile on his lips. As his eyes fastened on Gabrielle, she felt her heart skip a beat. "I've been waiting on you, Dr. Grinage. You're hardly late, but I'd hoped you show up early. How're you feeling? Did you sleep well?"

Gabrielle wrung her hands together. "I'm feeling fine and I slept very well, thank you."

Except for when you invaded my dreams and I was more than willing to surrender to your sexual desires.

"This is the last day at sea, and we make port in the morning. We can expect the clinic to be bustling with the crewmembers we need to recheck. As the day wears on, the patient list will probably completely dwindle down since everyone will want to enjoy the last night on the ship."

"Thanks for the heads-up. Listen, I need to know how to handle something. As you know, my family lives in Galveston, and I'd like to see them for a while. Can they board the ship to visit with me in my suite, or will I be able to go to my parents' home?"

"It'll probably be best if you go home. The ship will undergo a major overhauling during and after disembarkation and cleaning crews will be everywhere. All staff has to be back aboard the ship by 2:00 p.m., and we set sail for our alternate destinations at 5:30 p.m."

"I know we get into Galveston around 7:00 a.m. I'm dying to see my family. I've missed them so much."

Cameron looked closely at Gabrielle. "Are you homesick enough for this to be the end of the line for you?"

Gabrielle shook her head. "No way! I miss my family, but I love my job. I've never lived far away from them, but I'm all grown up now."

Relieved by her response, Cameron chuckled. "Yes, you are that. Do you have an apartment in Galveston?"

"I own a home there, but I leased it out for a year." She clasped her hands together in an excited gesture. "I'm looking forward to the next itinerary. I've always wanted to visit Jamaica."

"The entire Caribbean is beautiful, but our ship has the best destinations. Not many ships alternate itineraries biweekly. Fleets normally have one course for an entire season."

"So I've heard." She scratched her head, looking a bit perplexed. "About last night, I hope we didn't ruin our friendship. I want you in my life, and if I can only have you as a friend, so be it. I'll take you as a friend in a heartbeat."

Cameron looked concerned. "Am I hearing regrets about the passion we shared last night? I hope my ears are deceiving me. We'll get this all figured out. But know this—you have my friendship in the bank. But I want more than—"

"Morning, Dr. Quinn and Dr. Grinage! Good to see you both." Marjorie sniffed the air. "I don't smell coffee. Did you two just make it in?"

Cameron grimaced. "I got here first, but I had other things on my mind. I'll get the coffee going." He got up and walked to the breakroom.

Marjorie laughed. "I bet I know what's on his mind. Dr. Quinn is so attracted to you he can't even think straight. Each time I see you together, I see a love connection."

"Let's not go there," Gabrielle suggested. "Cameron and I are coworkers sharing a few social events together."

"So are Tristan and me. But I'm willing to bet my last dollar we'll be lovers before we finish our next itinerary. I think of him constantly, intimately. The man is hot."

Gabrielle laughed. "He *is* definitely hot, and I'm not talking about Tristan." She gave Marjorie a knowing smile. "I've had some intimate thoughts of my own about Cameron…"

A guest walked into the clinic, which immediately silenced Gabrielle.

Once the lady was signed in and had filled out an information sheet, she was assigned an exam room. Both Cameron and Gabrielle read what the nurse had written on the complaint sheet. It seemed she had a simple case of the sniffles; a runny nose but no cough.

"I'll take her, Cameron. You can get one of the men who just came in. I'm sure they'd rather have a male doctor," she joked.

Cameron winked. "Not if the female doctor is as beautiful as you."

Gabrielle introduced herself to the patient who was in her mid-thirties, according to the paperwork she'd filled out. "What seems to be the problem, Mrs. Cannon? By the way, I'm sorry you don't feel well, but you look really good."

Mrs. Cannon shrugged, forcing a weak smile. "Thank you, Dr. Grinage, but I feel like crap. I've had a runny nose since yesterday. I can't seem to get it under control even with the allergy-cold medicine I've been taking."

Using her stethoscope, Gabrielle listened to the patient's lungs. When she didn't hear anything unusual, she took her temperature. She then checked her heart and blood pressure, standard procedures for all patients who were medically assessed.

"The good news is that you don't have a fever and your blood pressure is excellent. However, when I checked your glands, they felt a bit swollen. The runny nose may be the beginning of the flu, but we can't treat you for anything that isn't manifesting. I suggest you see your own physician as soon as you get home. And you should stop taking the cold medicine since we don't have a definite diagnosis yet."

Mrs. Cannon got to her feet. "I'll follow your orders, and thanks for your time. How much will this visit set me back?"

"Not a single penny. I merely did an assessment. It was a pleasure meeting you." Gabrielle extended her hand to Mrs. Cannon, who shook it gently.

Over an hour later Gabrielle walked into Cameron's office and took a seat. "Mrs. Cannon's medical problem was an easy one. How are the crewmembers?"

Cameron smiled. "Everything looks good, so far. We haven't checked everyone, but we're making progress."

"That's good to know." She sighed with contentment. "I can honestly say I've enjoyed my first sailing. The days have flown by like wildfire. I can't wait to see my family, and I hope everyone shows up. I emailed my brothers and asked them to please come by."

"I'm sure they won't disappoint you. My parents will be in Europe, so I don't plan to go to their place in Houston. Besides, it's too far for such a short time. I hope you have a grand time with your family—I almost envy you."

Surprised by Cameron's comment, Gabrielle arched an eyebrow. "*Envy* is such a strong word. I hope you don't mean that."

"No, I didn't. I said *almost*. I don't see my sisters as often as I'd like to, and we don't stay in close contact."

Gabrielle appeared concerned. "Why not?"

He shrugged. "I write them emails, but weeks go by before they respond. I didn't mean to hurt your feelings. I should've made myself clearer."

"I'm not hurt." She smiled. "Why don't you come home with me? I know my family would love to meet you. I've already emailed them about you."

"You have? How deep into details about us did you go?"

"Nothing personal, mostly job-related stuff. I mentioned how kind you've been to me."

Since he hadn't even commented on her offer to join her family, she wished she hadn't gone there. Gabrielle rushed to her feet. "I'd better check to see what's happening up front."

Cameron saw tears in her eyes, and he couldn't help wondering what had brought them on. He hit his forehead with an open palm, when he realized he hadn't responded to her invite.

Once Gabrielle had come out of the bathroom from repairing her tear-stained face, Cameron went to her and said he'd love to meet her family. She'd barely been able to hide how happy she was that he would join her.

Emma Grinage had warm mahogany skin and silky mixed gray and black hair. Slender and classy, she stood at five-five. She hugged her daughter tightly in the foyer, like it was the last time she'd see her. "Let me look at you, my precious girl. It appears you're being treated very well. Love the suntan."

Emma realized that she needed to meet and greet her daughter's friends. They'd already met her husband, Ross.

Slipping one arm around Gabrielle's shoulder, Emma extended her hand to each of the guests. "Welcome to the Grinage home. It's a pleasure for my husband and me to have you. I'll leave the other introductions to Gabrielle."

Over six foot three, Ross Grinage was an attractive man, with bone-white hair, blue eyes and fair skin. He had met everyone at the dock, so Gabrielle presented her

brothers Ryan, Christopher and Jonathan to her shipmates. One brother was missing in action, but he was
coming. Maxwell had given his sister his word; she'd
never known him to go back on it.

"You all will meet Maxi when he arrives," Gabrielle said.

Emma and Ross led the way into the interior of their
clean-as-a-whistle, modest, beautifully furnished beach
house. They lived closer to the Gulf of Mexico than was
safe during hurricane season, but they'd been blessed
over the years. Some minor damages had occurred to
their property, but nothing significant. The beach house
had been in their family for generations. They'd raised
their children in a large two-story home on Galveston
Island, but had moved into the beach house after the
last offspring had flown the coop. Gabrielle had been
the last bird to leave the nest.

"Where's our baby girl?" Maxwell's deep baritone
voice echoed throughout the place. "Come and give big
brother his hugs, baby sis. I've missed you."

Gabrielle ran back to the foyer and leaped into
Maxwell's arms, kissing his face and the top of his
head, hugging him warmly. "Good to see you, Maxi.
I've missed you."

"I've missed you more," he said.

The brunch in Gabrielle's honor had been prepared
by her mother, who loved to whip up all sorts of reci-
pes while she puttered around in her kitchen. She had
prepared a light Sunday brunch of both breakfast and
lunch items and lots of cut up fresh fruits.

In the spacious, newly remodeled kitchen, Gabrielle
slipped up behind her mother and encircled her waist
with her arms. "Thanks for allowing me to bring my

friends home and for fixing a meal on such a short notice. Out of the blue, I asked Cameron to come home with me and meet my family. He's a great man. Marjorie and Tristan were also happy to be invited."

"Everyone seems happy," Emma responded. "Dr. Quinn sure is a handsome devil. I wonder if he's a spiritual man. Are you two soul mates?"

Gabrielle looked thoughtful. "I think on some level we are, but we're both very cautious. We're building a relationship from the ground up. He was hurt by a romantic relationship with a colleague, just like I was. It's hard to regain trust."

"Yes, it is very hard indeed. But we can't go around mistrusting everyone we meet. That would be unfair. You were taught to be forgiving, so I can't see that standing in your way. You have forgiven, haven't you?"

Gabrielle appreciated her mother not saying Jordan's name when she didn't have to. "I think I have. But then I have these awful flashbacks and sometimes they're haunting. But they could be warnings of some kind. I don't know why I recall all the ugliness in my life."

"Maybe it's because you haven't forgiven yourself. You may blame yourself for something you think you should've had control over. And you had your misgivings from the beginning. You should always listen to that little voice inside your head, because it knows what it's talking about."

"I think you may be right. I've taken too much of the blame for what happened instead of squarely placing it where it belongs. Thanks, Mom. I'll take this little talk with me when I go."

Emma knew she'd said the right thing, and she was

sure her daughter would take heed. "By the way, where are Dr. Quinn, Tristan and Marjorie?"

Gabrielle sighed deeply. "The guys are outside playing basketball with Dad and the boys. Marjorie is watching. Cameron is athletic, so I'm sure he'll do well against the Grinage clan."

"When are they going to learn that no man is measured solely on his athletic abilities?" Emma shook her head. "You'd better go tell everyone to come to the dining room."

Gabrielle looked around the table and smiled. She was so pleased that all of her brothers had made it home. She was also happy that they hadn't grilled Cameron about anything personal yet. They didn't know that she had a major attraction to him—and she wanted to keep it that way. Marjorie and Tristan seemed to be enjoying themselves, too.

She waved her fork in the air. "You guys should join the medical team on the *Parisian Paradise*. You'd love it."

"That good, huh?" Maxwell asked. "Glad you're enjoying your job."

Gabrielle looked at her mother. "Mom, thanks for all this great food. You prepared all of our favorites for brunch."

Maxwell looked over at his sister. "I know you're not surprised by it. She cooks like this every time we get together."

He then looked hard at Cameron, assessing him through slitted eyes. "Dr. Quinn, I get the feeling I know you, but I can't figure it out."

"We're on the same page. Weren't you in the U.S. Navy?"

Maxwell snapped his fingers. "That's it. We sailed together on the USS *Solstice*. Man, it's been a long time. I'm glad we're meeting up again. It's hard to believe that you and Gabrielle are working side by side, the way we did years ago."

Gabrielle looked on in utter amazement. If her brother knew Cameron, and liked him, that was half the battle. Maxwell was her fiercest protector. Seeing the men getting along so well finally allowed her to sit back and relax.

Yeah, she thought, sometimes being the only female sibling in her family wasn't always easy.

Chapter 8

Good times had passed by much too quickly, Gabrielle thought, leaning on the balcony railing outside her cabin. Watching the *Parisian Paradise* set sail from its home port was exciting, yet kind of sad. Leaving behind her family wasn't easy, but she was comforted in knowing she'd more than likely see them next Sunday when they returned to the Port of Galveston. The first port of call on the new itinerary was Montego Bay, Jamaica.

As soon as the ship was a fair distance from the port, Gabrielle went back inside. The phone rang, and she rushed across the room to pick up the receiver.

"Hey, it's Cameron. I want to know if you're okay. I saw how hard it was on you to leave your home and say goodbye to the family. How're you doing?"

"Teary but I'm good. I won't stop missing my family, but I need to curb the sadness."

"It's perfectly normal. I miss my family, too, more than I tend to let on." He paused for a moment. "Up to having some company?"

Gabrielle's heart fluttered. "I was thinking of also asking Marjorie and Tristan to come by. Would you mind?" She knew she was using the couple as a safeguard, but she didn't know any other way to handle the sudden change in her relationship with Cameron.

"Wouldn't mind at all."

"Great. Can you give me a half hour or so?"

"I certainly can. See you then."

What seemed like the perfect solution to her slight distress was simply a bad idea. She and Cameron had yet to figure out their relationship, but bad idea or not, she wanted to see him. Becoming romantically involved was one thing, but they also had to think about how to handle it publicly.

Gabrielle hadn't expected Cameron to be overtly attentive to her at her parents' place because it would've caused too much curiosity. But she had seen the meaningful looks he had given her. Knowing her brothers as well as she did, she knew they would've tried their best to satisfy their nosiness. The last thing she would've guessed was that Cameron and Maxwell had been shipmates years ago. The more they'd talked about the experience, the more they bonded. Yes, the entire time at home had gone smoothly.

Emma had taken to Cameron instantly and had found him to be very sincere and charming. She had told her daughter to give herself permission to love Dr. Quinn.

"Mom is so wise. She's right about listening to what our little voice inside says." There was a knock on the door, and Gabrielle hustled to greet her guests.

She opened the door to Marjorie. "Where's Tristan?" she queried.

"He'll be along soon. He had to handle a couple of things."

"Have a seat in the living room. Cameron won't be long in getting here."

Gabrielle took a deep breath. "Girl, you have no idea how much that sexy doctor turns me on. Hiding my feelings for him can't get any harder than it is. We haven't defined our relationship, but I want him in so many ways. Yet I'm extremely afraid of getting hurt."

Marjorie looked closely at Gabrielle. "You're in love with him, aren't you? Your eyes are a dead giveaway. I'd know that look anywhere."

The two women sat down on the sofa.

"I don't know about that," Gabrielle fibbed. "The potential to love him is great. He's a good man. If love claims us, you'll be the first to know."

Yet she knew that she'd love to shout out her love for Cameron from the top deck of the ship.

Is a confession of love imminent?

It was so hard for Gabrielle to sit still, especially when she felt jittery. Just thinking of Cameron made her feel hyper. Any second now, he would show up. Whatever look she had in her eyes would only deepen in his presence. She'd already admitted to herself that she loved Cameron—but she was both ecstatic and fearful about it. "Would you like something to drink?"

"7-Up will be fine if you have it."

Gabrielle's eyes lit up when she heard a knock at the door. He was here, but she couldn't put her arms around him and savor the taste of his full lips. It had been too long since their first kiss. She couldn't help wondering if it would happen again before he left.

Pull it together, she told herself. *Marjorie already suspects your feelings for Cameron.*

Then Gabrielle thought it could be Tristan at the door. In the next instant, she dismissed the idea. Her heart wouldn't be beating double-time if Cameron wasn't outside her door.

She made eye contact with Marjorie. "I'll get the door, then I can take care of your drink."

Gabrielle ran to the cabin door and swung it back. Cameron looked like he had walked out of an advertisement in a magazine. The man was so sexy and *GQ*. How could one man have so many different wonderful attributes? Her heart had hit the nail right on the head. Cameron Quinn stood toe-to-toe with her, and her desire to devour him increased tenfold.

Standing on tiptoes, she kissed his cheek. "Glad you're here. It's nice to see you."

His lips briefly grazed hers. "The feeling is mutual. Has anyone else arrived?"

"Marjorie is here. I was getting her something to drink. Come on in and make yourself comfortable. Do you want anything to sip?" She noticed the deep disappointment in his eyes. Had he also hoped they'd share a few passionate kisses alone?

Cameron moved into the foyer, smiling devilishly. "I'll take a Sprite. If you'd been one of the choices in hot drinks," he whispered, "I would've definitely chosen you."

Blushing heavily and thrilled by his flirtatious remark, Gabrielle led Cameron into the living room. "You two get caught up on the latest shipboard gossip. When I get back, I'd love to hear it all, too."

Cameron and Marjorie laughed. Then the doorbell summoned Gabrielle once again.

Cameron leaped to his feet just as Gabrielle moved toward the door. "I'll get it for you. It's probably Tristan. We *are* expecting him."

Gabrielle saw that Marjorie was fidgeting and anxious to see Tristan.

"I'm definitely expecting him," Marjorie whispered. "He's all I've thought about in his absence. Gabrielle, I'm glad you invited him and me. Thank you."

Gabrielle smiled knowingly. "You're welcome."

Tristan's personality was as bubbly as ever as he greeted his friends. He then headed straight for the seat next to Marjorie, leaning in to kiss her cheek. "We're becoming the fab four. Gabrielle, I had a great time at your parents' home. The food was excellent."

"It was," Marjorie seconded. "Mr. and Mrs. Grinage are superb hosts. And your good-looking brothers must have women chasing them day and night."

That comment got Marjorie a jealous look from Tristan.

"Thanks for the kind words. My parents love to host events. As for my brothers, they're not playboys at all. They're still too busy with their professional obligations to get involved in exclusive relationships. They date occasionally, but I'm not sure if they'll ever marry."

"Aren't your parents pushing for someone to get married and give them grandkids?" Marjorie asked.

"Actually, no. Our parents are content to let us lead our own lives in the same way they did," Gabrielle explained. "If we need them, they lend an ear. Otherwise, they butt out. Is there anything you guys want to do for fun?"

"What about a game of Monopoly or Taboo?" Tristan suggested.

Everybody shouted out for Taboo.

Gabrielle excused herself to get the game out of the closet. Seconds later, Cameron came up behind her. As he turned her around, he pulled her into the bathroom and into his arms, his strong physique taking her over completely. Then his mouth crushed down over hers in the most thrilling kiss of all. Despite knowing they shouldn't be doing this with company right around the corner, she couldn't bear to tear herself away. His kiss and his arms being wrapped tightly around her was exactly what she had been longing for.

Cameron looked deep into Gabrielle's eyes. "I guess we'd better get back out there. I just couldn't wait any longer to hold you close to me and kiss you."

Gabrielle wished that her cheeks weren't stained with color and that heat hadn't inflamed her body.

All that from just one kiss.

Two hours later Marjorie and Tristan got to their feet.

"We've had a blast, but it's time to go. Let's do dinner again soon," Tristan said to Gabrielle and Cameron.

Cameron nodded. "We'll try to work it into our schedules. Even though the clinic closes for lunch and dinner, Gabrielle and I are on call after it closes for the evening. But I'm glad Phillip and Patrick are on duty now, so we can get together more easily."

At the door of her cabin, Gabrielle and Cameron wished the couple a pleasant night.

Once the door was closed, Cameron turned to Gabrielle. "Mind if I stay awhile longer?"

As usual, her heart rate was all worked up. "I'd love for you to stay." *My head tells me to send you away but my heart tells me otherwise.*

Without further query, Cameron moved back into the living room and sat on the sofa.

"Can I get you anything else?"

He grinned. "All I want is more time in your company. Come sit with me."

Readily obeying his gentle command, Gabrielle glided over to the sofa and seated herself very close to him. A whiff of his cologne caused her to draw in a deep breath. He always smelled so refreshingly manly.

Cameron settled his arms around Gabrielle's shoulder. "I owe you an apology."

Gabrielle looked baffled. "For what?"

"I didn't answer your question right away about me coming home with you. I was caught up in the things you might've told your family about us. But I saw the tears in your eyes when you left the office, and that's when I realized I'd hurt your feelings by not responding. I'm sorry."

Gabrielle wanted to deny that it had affected her. But he had apologized and she should graciously accept. "Yes, I got teary-eyed. I was just disappointed that you hadn't answered me. Luckily, everything worked out perfectly and I'm over my earlier reaction."

"Thank you for not holding grudges." He stroked the side of her face with his index finger. "I'd like to hear some music. What about you? Is it okay if I load a couple of CDs?"

Gabrielle smiled. "Music makes the world go around. Help yourself."

He lifted his body from the sofa and strode over to the entertainment center. He selected a CD and loaded it into the changer. Extending his hands to Gabrielle, he asked her to share a dance with him. He gently helped her up and brought her right into his arms.

The song was slow and tantalizing as they held each other close. She felt like clouds had huddled beneath her feet as he slowly whirled her around the confined space. Laying her head against his chest came so natural for her, and she fit against his body perfectly.

Would their naked bodies be a perfect fit, too?

She didn't know how she knew, but she felt sure they would.

They danced to all nine slow songs before Gabrielle returned to the sofa.

Cameron went to fully stack the CD changer so there would be no more interruptions. "Anything you'd like to hear?"

"LeAnn Rimes is one of my favorite singers. I haven't listened to her in a while."

"You got it, babe. I'll throw a little Beyoncé on for me. She gets things smoking."

Unable to stop herself, Gabrielle began analyzing his remarks, wondering if he knew she was already smoldering beneath her clothes. She hadn't been in his arms this long ever and she hadn't wanted him to let her go, but the heat was on and she needed to cool down. Things were smoking between them even without the music. Every time he touched her, he left her feeling hot all over. She even got hot just thinking of him.

As LeAnn Rimes belted out Bette Middler's iconic

"The Rose," Gabrielle got to her feet and walked over to pull Cameron into another slow dance. "I love that song. It's so deep."

"It *is* beautiful!" He kissed the top of her head. "As beautiful as you are." Lowering his head, he gave her a mind-blowing kiss that sent her reeling into depths unknown. If he had his way, he'd kiss her all night long.

"How Do I Live" by LeAnn Rimes came on next and it ruined her mood. She fought the darkness, but knew she couldn't win a war bigger than she was. She couldn't stop her tears when she remembered how many nights she'd played that song after she and Jordan had broken up and she had cried her heart out. She'd asked herself so many times how she could live without Jordan, but none of that was applicable now. Living without him and letting go of their twisted relationship was the best choice she'd ever made. Jordan was a tainted piece of her history.

Gabrielle knew that the same song would definitely apply to Cameron. She'd already asked herself countless times how she would go on if his feelings for her didn't develop as deeply as the ones she already had for him. Mad at herself for asking for the song to be played, she fiercely but silently admonished herself.

To add injury to insult, "The Heart Never Forgets" then came on. It was another song Gabrielle heavily related to. She felt like doubling over from the agony of what her heart hadn't forgotten, what it would never forget.

Removing herself from Cameron's warm embrace, Gabrielle slowly walked back to the sofa and dropped down onto it with a heavy heart. The evening was over for her and she hated it. Once she got into this kind of funk, it took her a long time to bounce back.

With a look of concern on his face, Cameron sat down next to Gabrielle and put his arm around her in a consoling manner. "Something happened. Want to talk about it?"

She shook her head. "It won't do any good."

"Try me. You might be surprised," Cameron said.

"The last two songs brought back bad memories." She turned to look him square in the eye. "I shouldn't have had you play them. It's been a long time since I've heard the CDs, and I didn't know I'd still feel so hurt."

Cameron squeezed her shoulders. "What can I do to get you back in a good mood?"

"You should probably just go. This mood isn't going to improve."

"And if I refuse to go?"

Her eyes narrowed as she burned her gaze into his. "That's not an option, Cameron. I need to be alone."

"Why? You said you're over your past hurts. What's keeping you from trusting again? You can trust me, Gabrielle—I'm not going to hurt you."

"You may not intend to, but it can happen regardless."

"Tell me your fears." He gently stroked the length of her hair with one hand, massaging her shoulders with the other. "You can trust me to understand, Gabby."

Her eyes leveled on him again. "I am over the past hurts, but I still can't forget them. I can't go into another relationship with blinders on. You're the perfect package, the perfect ten all women love to talk about. But we're shipmates, and we work together. If we continue down the path we're on, and you suddenly pull back, it'll be so awkward for me around the clinic. I don't think we can survive a working relationship *and* a romantic one."

Cameron frowned. "What if you're the one to pull back, like you're doing now? Don't you think it'll be awkward for me, too?"

Gabrielle shrugged her shoulders. "I hadn't thought of that. I'm too busy protecting my own heart. Somehow men don't seem to get as devastated as women. Why's that?"

He shook his head. "Not true. Men hurt deeply, too. They just hide their broken hearts and they don't share it with anyone. I think we're more able to move on rather than get depressed."

"My heart wasn't hurt due to love. I thought I loved this guy, but I never even liked him. I failed to go with my first impression of him and it backfired on me. If I can't protect my own heart, who in the hell can?"

He eyed her with deep curiosity. "Can you trust me to also protect it? It's obvious that we're deep into each other, so why can't things just flow naturally? Stop thinking about what might happen because it may never occur. I don't toy with the hearts of women."

"Like I said, you're the perfect package. But that doesn't change that we're coworkers. Been there and done that."

Cameron was bitterly disappointed in the way things were going, yet he felt that he couldn't give up on her, not when he wanted to be with her the way he did. "I feel a very special connection to you, a strong one; the kind I've never felt before. Will we go the distance? Only time can tell, but if we don't give it a chance, we'll never know."

Gabrielle shook her head. "I just don't think it's that simple."

"Will you give me the chance to show you I'm an upstanding, honorable man? I can't guarantee what may or may not happen for us. There are no guarantees in love and life."

The sincerity in Cameron's eyes weakened her position. "I can try my best to give you a chance to do that, but what are we going to do about our relationship publicly? How do we handle the pressure of working together?"

Cameron smiled. "We've already been very public. Others have seen me holding your hand. Let them draw their own conclusions. There are no ship rules against fraternization, so there's not a single reason we can't operate in public as a couple just like others. Take time to think about it."

Gabrielle kissed Cameron lightly on the mouth before she got up from the sofa. She strolled over to the balcony door, opened it and went outside, where she hoped to find the brightest star to make a wish upon. She also wanted the breezy air to help clear her head.

Gabrielle went into deep thought. *Let things go with the flow,* she told herself. *Like Cameron said, there are no guarantees in life and in love.* She dashed away hot tears with her fingertips. There came a time when a woman had to take what she wanted and accept that the consequences may not turn out to be the desired ones. She wanted Cameron in her life for however long it lasted. To deprive herself the company of the man she'd already fallen deeply for served no purpose.

Opening the door, she poked her head inside. "Come join me. It's breathtaking."

"I'd love to."

Cameron had stayed behind to give Gabrielle time alone to sort out her feelings. He hoped she'd give him a chance to prove to her that he wasn't a heartless man. Her pain was much deeper than he'd expected. No matter how hard she'd tried to hide it, she couldn't. The road might be rougher than he'd imagined, but he was used to navigating in the worst of conditions. All he knew was that she was worth whatever time he'd spend trying to break her away from the past.

Outside on the balcony, where stars shone brightly overhead, Cameron stood facing Gabrielle. Her back was against the metal railing as he gazed into her eyes. The desire to kiss her permeated his entire being, making him weak with longing. Cupping her face between his hands, he tilted her head slightly. His heart beat like a jackhammer, and at the same time his breathing fluctuated between shallow and ragged. Cameron's head came down slowly. Then his lips tenderly sampled the sweetness of her lusciously ripe mouth.

As his lips undulated hungrily over hers, Gabrielle suddenly felt her tension completely collapse. Pressing her hand onto the back of his head, she held it in place, guiding his full lips back to hers, kissing him fervently. Wild, zinging sensations sailed through her, making her want Cameron in the worst way.

Gabrielle pulled her head back and their eyes connected. "Should we do this again?"

A familiar question, she mused, the same one she'd asked herself over and over.

His smoky gaze embraced her, piercing her composure. "What do you think?"

"We're coworkers, Cameron. Is mixing labor and lust a good idea?"

"What I feel with you is so much stronger than lust. Should I just continue to feel tortured around you?"

"Tortured?" Her eyebrows slanted. "What makes you feel that kind of agony?"

For a brief moment, Cameron closed his eyes. "Have you ever wanted something so badly that you thought you'd die if you couldn't get it? I feel tortured because I've imagined having you emotionally and physically since I first laid eyes on you."

Gabrielle's eyelashes fluttered. She knew exactly what it felt like to desire forbidden fruit. The need to taste it was horribly tortuous. She turned her back. "Somebody please help us," she whispered.

Help Cameron and me get through passion's raging storm without losing ourselves to mere sexual gratification and the possibility of never experiencing anything else. Was sex worth the tough sacrifices? No, she concluded, it wasn't. But as he'd said, this wasn't about sex. This was about deep feelings and the fear of rejection and pain. *I have to trust him because he's already in my blood. I've already compromised my heart.*

Gabrielle knew she wanted more than sex with Cameron. And she no longer questioned how much more—she knew she wanted a close and personal relationship with him.

To silence the fear he saw in her eyes, Cameron kissed her, curving his tongue around hers, probing deeply. Increasing the pressure on her lips, he took full advantage of her sweet mouth. His erection felt as if it was bursting through his pants. Placing his hands on her buttocks, he brought her in closer to him, wanting her to feel him.

Her body hungered for the feel of him nesting deeply inside her. Visuals of him making love to her had her lathered up. His sex grinding into her hips increased her desire for him. If only she could find the courage to reach down and stroke him through his clothing. But that kind of bravado wasn't in her.

The vision of tasting Cameron's entire body caused Gabrielle to gasp wantonly. She wouldn't protest one iota if he took her love-starved body right there on the balcony. Making love to him consumed both her daytime fantasies and nighttime dreams. She'd awaken in the middle of the night bathed in sweat, disappointed that he wasn't lying beside her. Her body craved his.

As though he had read her mind, he lowered his body onto the chaise and brought her down on top of him. As he recaptured her lips, his hands hotly roved over her hips and the back of her thighs. Cameron wished she didn't have on pants, since they restricted access to the moist center of her core.

Raising herself off him, Gabrielle smoothed her clothes. It was one thing for her to sunbathe nude on the balcony, but as much as she wanted to have him make love to her right here, she felt the need to practice caution. Taking hold of his hand, she helped him get up. She slowly walked into the cabin and over to the alcove where her bed was.

After lying down on the mattress, she motioned for Cameron to lie with her.

He lay alongside her and rested his head next to hers. Taking his hand, she guided it under her shirt and toward her braless breasts. The stunned look in his eyes pleased her, but the throbbing response of his sex made her crazy with desire.

As Cameron moved his hand back and forth between her breasts, tenderly squeezing and massaging them, Gabrielle felt as if she was ready to explode into a wild orgasm. His hands felt moist and hot on her tingling flesh, and she turned her head from side to side to try to control her roller-coaster emotions. She wanted him to take her right then. She wasn't all that experienced in lovemaking, but she knew what turned on a man and what worked for her.

Lifting his head from Gabrielle's chest, Cameron turned up on his side. His eyes went to the zipper on her pants just before his hands reached down and lowered it. Sliding his hand inside her silk panties, he explored her intimate zone with gentleness. Taking a deep breath, he parted her legs and slid his hand between them. Without any resistance from her, he inserted a single digit deep inside her. The pooling moisture around his finger let him know she wanted him. As she raised her hips to remove her pants, he watched her intently.

Prepared to stop all aggressive actions if she sent off such a signal, Cameron studied her closely as he slowly stripped away her panties. Nothing about this moment would be rushed. He didn't know how much time they had, but he planned to ask her to sleep in his arms all night long, whether they were on call or not. It didn't matter which cabin they chose.

A loud warning signal suddenly went off in Gabrielle's head, and she sat straight up. She couldn't help thinking about Jordan and the horrific damage he'd done to her heart. "I can't do this," she whispered, struggling with her emotions. "I'm too afraid."

Cameron smoothed his hand over her hair. After pulling the comforter back, he covered her. "It's okay. We don't have to. We should probably concentrate on getting to know each other through and through. I want you more than I can express, but I want you to be comfortable."

Gabrielle didn't know what to make of his comments. It sounded as if she was being rejected in a supersensitive way. There was no way she could go forward even if she wanted to. They both had to know it was right for them, but she didn't feel devastated by that because of the sincere way in which Cameron had made his feelings known. Perhaps he had actually stopped her from making an even bigger mistake than she'd made before.

Gabrielle sighed deeply. "I'm sorry I couldn't go through with this."

"Don't worry about it." He kissed her forehead. In tune with her emotions, he went about the necessary task of redressing her, kissing her every few moments.

"Thank you, Cameron. You're very understanding."

"I'd like to think so. I'm sorry I let things go this far. I feel like I've taken advantage of you, I'm your superior and this shouldn't have happened. I should've listened to you, but all I thought of was what I needed. Can you forgive me?"

She moved forward and leaned her forehead against his. "Nothing to forgive. We simply moved too fast. It may be the wrong direction for us despite how I feel about you."

His eyes connected with hers. "How do you feel?"

Her eyes filled with tears. "I should plead the Fifth, but I won't. I have strong feelings for you, Cameron. I've even imagined myself in love with you."

His heart nearly stopped. His love for her was hardly imagined. It was true and pure.

Pulling her head down, he guided it onto his chest. "I don't want you to live with regret. I want you more than you can imagine. And like you, I felt the timing was wrong. Your earlier reactions to those songs let me see how vulnerable you still are. But let me spend the night and just hold you. I want to be here. I love you, Gabrielle."

Her heart pounded away at his confession. She wanted to tell him she loved him, too, but she'd said her feelings were imagined. "Please stay. And I'm doing this solely for me." She smiled through her tears. "I wanted us to make love. I wasn't just grandstanding or being a tease."

"I know, sweetheart. I never thought of you like that."

"Thanks." She put her head down for a moment. As she raised her head, her eyes were full of some emotion Cameron couldn't discern. "I'm afraid I gave in to my fear of being hurt again. I'm a woman who thought I was in love with someone I didn't even like. I was a dreamer all during the brief affair."

Cameron looked deeply into her eyes. "What do you mean?"

"In the beginning, after I learned to ignore the nagging warnings, I dreamed of what I thought he and I could be together. I daydreamed about how it seemed we were. His tenderness turned into carelessness, and his respect for me dwindled rapidly. Before long I was cringing at his senseless machismo and his desire to control me."

Cameron squeezed her hand. "I'm sorry, Gabrielle."

She shook her head. "My dreams eventually turned to nightmares and I could finally see exactly how it was. The love he professed for me felt like hate." Her emotions spilled over and then she couldn't continue.

While wiping away her tears, she fought hard to compose herself. "I'll...be right...back." Gabrielle got out of bed and fled over to the dresser drawers, where she pulled out a pair of plain pajamas, then headed into the bathroom.

Minutes passed but Cameron was still stunned by Gabrielle's heartbreaking story. Stripping down to his briefs, he slid into bed, knowing for sure he had to be there for her.

Dressed in her pajamas now, Gabrielle slid into bed next to Cameron and laid her head on his chest. "I desperately need you to hold me."

Encouraged by Gabrielle's request and glad she was more composed, Cameron wrapped his arms around her. He gave her a staggering kiss. "Sleep sweetly. I'll be right here. I hope this is the first night of endless ones."

Gabrielle smiled as she looked up into Cameron's eyes. "Sleeping in your arms is one of my dreams coming true."

"And it's one of mine. Close your eyes. I'll set the alarm. We're both on duty in the morning. If only the gossipmongers knew..."

Lying still, Gabrielle could feel Cameron's strong heartbeat. His cologne hadn't completely faded, and she inhaled its faint scent. For something that had begun so hot and heavy, it sure had cooled off in a hurry. She still wanted Cameron desperately, but it had to mean something deep. If it ever happened for them, she knew it would be amazing.

* * *

Bathed in sweat, Gabrielle woke at 3:00 a.m.

Sleeping next to Cameron was wonderful and terribly hard, all at the same time. She had hoped they'd come together during the night and indulge in light foreplay and petting, but for now she was still against them making wild, passionate love. He was sleeping like a baby and she'd slept fitfully. She hadn't shared a bed with a man in what seemed like eons. And never had she had the kind of uninhibited desire she constantly felt for Cameron.

Careful not to wake him, Gabrielle slipped out of bed and tiptoed into the bathroom. Without turning on the light, she squirted shower gel into the sink and mixed it with warm water to rinse off her sweaty body. On the way back to bed, she planned to get a fresh set of nightclothes.

Wouldn't it be nice if I had the nerve to go back to bed naked?

Gabrielle wondered how much time she and Cameron would spend together since they'd be at sea for nearly three days before docking in Montego Bay. Of course, they'd see each other at work, but she was thinking in intimate terms. With their cabins side by side, they certainly had easy access to one another.

Fumbling around for her deodorant, she found it and put some under her arms. She then dusted her body with scented powder, hoping it would keep her drier until they left for work. After leaving the bathroom, she fumbled around in the dresser drawer until she came up with a suitable nightgown, which she slipped on over her head.

Gabrielle tiptoed across the room but suddenly stubbed

her big toe against a chair. She put her hand over her mouth to stifle any sound. She hobbled the rest of the way and was as careful getting back into bed as she'd been slipping out. Cameron was still out cold.

Chapter 9

Cameron awakened, and the first thing his eyes zeroed in on was Gabrielle sleeping. She looked so peaceful, and he held back the desire to outline her beautiful features with his fingers and lips. She was a beautiful woman. He had regrets about how he'd handled things last night, but at the same time he was proud he'd righted the wrong. He didn't want her to think his interest in her was purely physical. Beauty would fade with time, but he didn't think what he felt for Gabrielle stood a chance of fading.

"Yes, sweetheart," Cameron whispered, "we'll take this slow. It'll be well worth it."

Cameron glanced at the clock radio. The alarm would go off shortly, at 7:00 a.m. Instead of waiting for the alarm, he turned it off then got dressed and slipped quietly out of her cabin.

Freshly showered, shaved and dressed in his whites, Cameron had used Gabrielle's key card to slip back into her place. He'd taken it to make sure she got up on time, since he'd silenced the alarm. He'd also had room service deliver breakfast for two to his suite, which he had brought along with him.

Cameron came over to the bed, where he expected to find Gabrielle still asleep. But she was gone. Then he heard the shower running. He did an about face and went into the kitchen to lay out the food and make coffee. He'd shared her bed last night, and he thought it only fitting that they share breakfast together.

Gabrielle stepped out of the bathroom while drying herself off. She'd been so disappointed that Cameron had slipped out on her before she'd wakened. She didn't know what it meant, but she couldn't stop trying to figure it out. If she hadn't wakened on her own, she would have been late to work since the alarm clock had been silenced. Why he'd turned off the alarm also had her perplexed.

Cameron snuck up behind Gabrielle and wrapped his arms around her, planting several kisses into her hair. "Good morning, Gabby! You look ravishing." Taking the towel from her hand, he finished drying her off.

Gabrielle was near speechless and terribly embarrassed. *Grow up,* she told herself. *You shared your bed with him last night.* All sorts of things had run through her mind about his absence, but here he was in the flesh. "You're dressed for work. How'd you get back in?"

"I took your key card off the table. I wanted to be here when you woke up, but you were already in the shower when I got back."

Although she was thrilled to see him back, she gave him a sly, wicked glance. "How can I be sure you didn't make a duplicate key card?"

"You know me better than that. It was just a onetime use. Breakfast is ready and so is the coffee. Slip on your robe so we can eat together."

Gabrielle couldn't hide her immense pleasure even if she had wanted to. Cameron was a kind, caring man, and it would serve her well not to try to second-guess his motives. She actually liked that he'd taken her key card—it had been a bold move.

She walked slowly to the table. She had slept well the second half of the night, but the first part had been difficult to get through. She plopped down in a chair, unable to believe what a nice breakfast Cameron had delivered. "Cameron's service or room service?"

Grinning, he winked at her. "A little bit of both. I brewed the coffee and room service prepared the meal. But I pulled it all together."

Cameron delivered Gabrielle her meal, setting before her the tray with the one over-medium egg, a slice of wheat toast and a bowl of cream of wheat. He filled two mugs with hot coffee and placed one in front of her. "Consider yourself served, babe."

She smiled brightly. "Thank you, Dr. Quinn. You've exceeded my expectations."

"Good! You don't have to do a thing to exceed mine. I'm already gone on you. I slept like a log in your bed—it's more comfortable than mine. Want to try it out tonight to compare?"

Gabrielle was moved by his offhand way of asking her to spend the night with him. "I'd love to try out yours." She suddenly looked flustered. "*Are* we moving too fast, Cameron?" She sighed. "I guess it's time to stop asking that question. We almost went all the way."

"Don't give it another thought. Sleeping in the same bed together and making love are totally different matters. In my opinion, we're taking it slow. I promised you we would."

Cameron took two bites of his egg then set down his fork. "What do you think of having an exclusive relationship? I don't want to date anyone else, and I don't want you to, either."

Gabrielle raised both eyebrows. "Oh, no, I can't commit to that. There are too many sexy men on the ship. I think that dating others now and then will be perfect for us."

Cameron's mouth fell agape. "Are you serious? I *really* read you wrong, didn't I?"

Gabrielle smiled tenderly. "No, you didn't. You read me just fine. But you'll have to get used to me dishing out a bit of shock value from time to time. I'd love for us to be exclusive, as long as it's good for both of us."

Cameron looked relieved as he blew out a steady stream of breath. He wanted to laugh but hadn't quite gotten over the initial shock of her statement. "Naughty but nice girl, huh? I can deal with it. I just hope you can handle it when my bad-boy side appears."

"Ooh, that sounds scary. Women say there's nothing like taming a bad boy. But let me tell you this, I am not into bad boys. So when that persona appears, I'll run the other way."

"I'm not a bad boy. Trust me." He grinned. "Anyway, I'll get the kitchen. I know housekeeping takes care of it, but I don't like taxing them since they do a lot of heavy labor."

Gabrielle nodded. "That's why I keep my place in tiptop shape. I don't want them to do anything I can do for myself. And don't worry, I got the kitchen."

"Whatever you say. I plan to go on down to the clinic, so I'll see you when you get there. Can I have a good-bye kiss?"

Cameron kneeled down in front of her and pulled her head down for his lips to meet up with hers. They kissed passionately. "See you shortly, Ms. Naughty But Nice. Your key card is back on the table where you put it."

"Thank you." She appeared doubtful. "I'm still worried about what we reveal about us in public. There's no way I can hide my strong attraction to you. Maybe I should wear sunglasses on duty."

Cameron cracked up. "We're no different from any other couple. If you haven't already noticed, you'll see couples in uniforms holding hands and even kissing. Stop worrying about it—we'll be fine. I can make a big announcement about us if you'd like."

Gabrielle looked horrified. "Please don't do that. We need to just act naturally, and I hope holding hands and kissing are natural acts for us." She laughed.

"They are. Turn off the alarms inside your pretty head. By the way, I'm trying to finagle some time to show you Montego Bay. I want to share it with you. Walk me to the door?"

Gabrielle got up and took Cameron's hand. "Thanks for last night. I wanted to make love to you…and I still do, but I'm glad we recognized the timing was wrong. Hopefully our time will come. See you in the clinic."

Hand in hand, they strolled to her cabin door, where he gave her a long kiss goodbye.

* * *

As Gabrielle looked into the mirror, she layered her long lashes with a couple of light strokes of sable-brown mascara. While slipping into her white uniform, she gave more thought to what had occurred last night. She and Cameron had been set to come together in a combustible way. Their emotional and physical fires had been stimulated to fever pitch, and an inexhaustible burning inferno would've consumed them had they made love. She was sure of it.

They'd been so close to the point of no return. *Should I be ashamed that it didn't work out?*

Gabrielle shook her head. "No, there's no shame in it. I wanted to make love to him, plain and simple. Do I regret the abrupt ending? Can't say that for sure, but it would've been more than an interesting time. I'm sure Cameron is a passionate, tender lover."

Gabrielle sat down on the sofa and pulled on her white work shoes. Loose-fitting clothing and comfortable footwear were a must in a clinic or hospital setting since they stood on their feet for hours on end. She took a last glance in the mirror at how she'd pulled herself together. Pleased with the outcome, she picked up her purse, key card and briefcase then headed for the door.

The entire staff was in the reception area when Gabrielle walked into the clinic. She greeted everyone and smiled. Then she noticed how everyone was smiling and grinning at her strangely. The looks on their faces said they knew something about her—and she was dying to know exactly what that was.

"Is everything okay?" Gabrielle asked anxiously.

"We're fine," Tristan said, "and from all indications, you're even better."

Gabrielle was wary now, wondering what Tristan was getting at. She looked him square in the eye. "If you have something to say, there's no need to dance around it. Spit it out."

"From what Dr. Quinn tells us, you guys are dating exclusively. Congratulations! You're a great couple." Tristan clapped his hands and the others joined in.

The claps felt like slaps to her face, and Gabrielle's complexion reddened.

"Thanks. I'll be in my office."

Without another word, Gabrielle walked past the staff, went into her private office and closed the door. She wanted to cry, but she'd have to settle for bawling inwardly. She was on duty. There'd be plenty of time for tears when she was alone in her cabin.

Other than the pounding in her head, she felt numb. The fact that Cameron hadn't discussed with her the announcement he'd made to the staff made her feel ill. It was like something Jordan would've done to show he was in control. She remembered how horrified she'd been when he'd mentioned making a big announcement. She'd clearly let him know it wasn't something she wanted him to do.

There was a knock on the door and Gabrielle lifted her head. She quickly composed herself. "Come in." Her voice sounded weak.

Cameron walked in and posted himself on the corner of Gabrielle's desk. As he leaned over to kiss her, she backed away. He stared at her in confusion.

"Wow, the temperature sure has dropped drastically. There's a subzero chill in the room. What's wrong?"

She rolled her eyes. "As if you don't know. How could you be so insensitive? I never dreamed you'd be this callous."

Cameron frowned. "Please tell me what you're talking about."

"Your big announcement about us to the staff! Why'd you do it when you already knew I didn't want you to?"

Cameron drew closer then took her hand. His beautiful eyes softened as he looked into her tear-filled gaze. "It's easier to put it out there than to allow gossip to run rampant. I don't want the staff whispering behind our backs. I can take it, but I'm not sure you're ready for the scrutiny. This was not an attempt to hurt or undermine you."

"It wasn't?" Gabrielle said, fuming.

"You asked me how we should handle it publicly, and I just ran with the ball."

Gabrielle glared at Cameron. "Do I look like a little girl to you? Do you see me as a damsel in distress? Because your assessment of what I can and can't handle sucks. I need you to treat me like the woman I am. You knew I would've opposed it because I said so earlier. But if you had tried, I'm sure you could've persuaded me that it was for the greater good. But now, I just feel betrayed."

Cameron's eyebrows angled. "Betrayed! That's a strong word to describe your feelings over what I did. I call it clearing our path. But since I'm catching hell, I may as well tell you that I also told the powers that be that we're dating. I don't see any reason to keep our love affair a secret. We've already been seen out and about together."

"So it's a love affair now? We didn't even make love."

Cameron held back a chuckle, fearful of offending her further. They hadn't made love physically, but their minds and bodies had had one hell of a passionate workout.

"It's whatever we want it to be, Gabby. Whether we're sleeping together or not, people will assume we are. The move I made doesn't have to be analyzed to death. Let's not complicate it."

Gabrielle put her elbows up on the desk and formed a steeple with her hands. "I guess you think I'm over-reacting?"

Cameron stroked his chin. "There's nothing to guess about. You've made yourself crystal clear. So where do we go from here? The invitation to spend the night in my cabin is a standing one, and nothing will happen that we don't want. That's my heartfelt promise to you. I love you."

"So how do I go out there and face our staff members?"

"They're all ecstatic about us as a couple. I wished you hadn't been approached about it before I could tell you. But are we still exclusive or not?"

You had me at first glance. "I need more time to think about what's happened. And you have to decide if you want to wait or not."

"My mind has never been in doubt about you. I'll wait. Take as long as you need, but just know that I'll be missing you every second." He stood. Walking over to her, he tilted her chin and gave her a mind-numbing kiss, one she wouldn't soon forget "I'll wait in my cabin for you tonight, after the clinic closes. If you're a no-show, I'll get the message."

Gabrielle softened at seeing him look so dejected.

She jumped up from her chair and threw her arms around Cameron's neck and kissed him passionately. "If I'm a no-show, you come to my cabin." With that said, she walked out, feeling a tad less anxious about facing the staff.

Outside in the hallway, Gabrielle blew out several streams of breath.

How close had she come to losing what she and Cameron had only just begun to build? She didn't know. Yet she *did* know she didn't want to lose him. He was right about the gossip and speculation. By telling the staff he'd taken the wind out of the sails of gossipers.

Gabrielle's worry about facing the staff was for nothing. When she stepped into the reception area, they were already whipped into action, and every chair and cubicle was filled with patients. Busy morning, she mused. Guests were perhaps getting checked out before docking in Montego Bay, where they'd want to explore and shop until they dropped. This was the busiest she'd ever seen the clinic…and it was so early in the cruise.

She got straight to work.

The hustle and bustle kept up. Cameron eventually had to call in backup nurses to get a handle on the onslaught, but was grateful nothing serious had come up. Minor aches and pains, cold symptoms and nausea, and seasickness were chief complaints.

It would be impossible to take a lunch break. As soon as one patient left, two or three more came. Outside of the crewmember scare last week, nothing like this had occurred in the clinic since she'd been working there. It was normally after forty-eight hours at sea that lots of guests showed up at the clinic.

* * *

Trying to get her headache under control, Gabrielle had just taken two painkillers and had lain down in bed with all the lights off.

From opening to closing time, the patient flow at the clinic had been nonstop. Gabrielle had to admit she was bone tired, but it had also been an excellent day of getting her feet wet in an array of medical procedures. She'd learned a lot this shift, more than on any other... and this was only the second week and second cruise out of the scheduled five months.

Gabrielle looked at the clock. She'd been off for over an hour now. Cameron hadn't given her a specific time to come to his cabin after the clinic closed, and she couldn't see herself making it anytime soon. Maybe she should ask for a rain check, but she knew that wouldn't go over well. Slowly, she sat up.

Seated on the side of the mattress, Gabrielle picked up the receiver and dialed the extension to Cameron's cabin. She listened to the first, second and third ring, hanging up on the fourth, before the voice mail clicked on. She wondered if he was on an emergency so she picked up the phone and called the operator. "This is Dr. Gabrielle Grinage. I was checking to see if there were any medical emergencies on board?"

"Not a one, Dr. Grinage. Is there something else I can do for you?"

"Nothing at all. Thank you. I was just trying to find out if Dr. Quinn needed assistance."

"Dr. Quinn was called to a special meeting with the administration board. I paged him to advise him of the closed-door session, but they're expected to adjourn soon."

Worried and upset, Gabrielle said goodbye and cradled the phone. The first thing she wondered was if the meeting had anything to do with the announcement Cameron had made about them. As she was second in command, she was also peeved that she hadn't been called to sit in. Maybe her absence meant it was about their romantic relationship—perhaps all the powers that be weren't okay with it.

The phone rang and Gabrielle snatched it up before it could ring a second time. "This is Dr. Grinage."

"Hey, naughty-but-nice girl, it's your naughty-by-night boyfriend. I had a meeting that came up at the last minute. Have you thought any more about coming to my cabin?"

"That's all I've been able to think about," she replied, thinking his *boyfriend* reference was so cute. "But I've got a headache. I just took a couple of pain pills, so give me some time.

"Not a problem. Give me an hour to shower and order food for us then I'll come to your cabin. I don't want to change your surroundings if you're not feeling well. Got anything in mind for dinner and dessert?"

"Sushi would be great. But avocado, California and cucumber rolls are about as brave as I'm willing to get. And a cup of steamed rice, please. I also have loads of green tea bags for us. No dessert for me."

"I've got your order memorized. Need anything stronger for your headache?"

"The pills are already working so I'm getting up to take a quick shower. See you soon."

Gabrielle was unsettled about whether she should or shouldn't ask Cameron about his meeting. It was probably just administrative stuff. But if so, why hadn't she been included?

She hoped this wasn't a man thing. If machismo had kept her out of this gathering, they'd hear an earful. She wasn't afraid to speak her mind, especially when it came to business.

"Men are men," she huffed, moving toward the bathroom, deciding not to address it.

Cameron would arrive soon, so she quickened her pace but was mindful of her slightly lingering headache. She combed her hair and left it to sweep across her shoulders. The perfect dress to wear came to mind and she smiled.

Rushing out of the bathroom, Gabrielle headed for the closet and pushed back clothing on the rack. "There you are."

She draped her body in a clinging eggshell-white crepe dress, breathing in the lingering, maddening scent of White Midnight perfume.

Gabrielle had only worn the dress once and was pleased by how well it fit her body. Giggling, she thought of pulling off a passable Caribbean accent to try out on Cameron, her new, self-appointed boyfriend.

Calypso songs were always playing in her home during her childhood and teen years, and the rhythmic sounds had consoled her on many nights. As an adult, the same music had grown close to her heart, saturating her imagination with an array of settings filled with love and eroticism and inspiring in her a desire to dance the night away.

She layered the same scented lotion and perfume by using it on her throat, behind her ears and on her wrist, all the while dreaming of the night ahead of her.

* * *

Gabrielle opened the cabin door to Cameron. Standing on tiptoes, she kissed him lightly. "Glad you're here. I was hoping you'd make it before the food delivery."

"I made it a point to get here before then." Bringing his hand from behind his back, he presented her with six yellow rosebuds nestled in a crystal vase. "I hope you like roses."

"Love them." She inhaled the scent of the blooms, which brought a huge smile to her face. "Thank you, Cameron. Come on in and have a seat."

Cameron took notice of the dress she wore. His heart had leapt at the sight of her curves outlined and hugged to perfection. "I love how good you look. Your dress is stunning, but not nearly as stunning as you."

"Thank you." Gabrielle wished she could prevent the schoolgirl blush that took over her face every time he said something sweet. She chalked it up as a good thing—no man had constantly said nice things to her like Cameron did.

He consulted his watch as he followed her into the living area. "The food is only minutes away. Are you hungry?"

Gabrielle shook her head. "I can't do a full entrée any justice."

He sat down on the sofa. "I sure can. I ordered a few other dishes."

She wrinkled her nose, dropping down next to him. "The sushi and rice will be enough for me."

Cameron hunched his shoulders. "That's fine. I don't expect you to eat a lot if you're not hungry. How's the headache?"

"It's completely gone, but before I go to bed, I'll take

two more painkillers. I'm glad I don't have the early-morning shift."

"That makes two of us."

She looked puzzled. "I saw your name on the early schedule."

He grinned. "I took care of it. I'm working the same shift as you tomorrow."

Gabrielle didn't know whether to smile or frown.

The employees were going to have a field day with their relationship. Hearing jokes about her and Cameron wouldn't sit well with her. The last thing she wanted was to be the butt of jokes. If it did happen, she'd already made up her mind to nip it in the bud. A knock on the door gratefully interrupted her train of thought.

"Excuse me." She rushed to the door and opened it to the delivery person.

The waiter came into the suite and went straight to the kitchen counter where he set down the trays. Knowing he was in an employee cabin, he didn't expect a tip, and he left as soon as the food was set down.

Gabrielle was glad Cameron had disappeared into the bathroom, so that the waiter wouldn't see them together. She quickly uncovered the food and laid out Cameron's order first. Then she took care of her own.

Cameron came out of the bathroom, wiping his hands on a towel then sat down at the table. "It looks good."

Gabrielle picked up a California roll with chopsticks. "I've never had the sushi, but I've heard from others that it's really delicious." She nibbled on it first. "It's good and fresh."

"Mind if I taste it?"

"Help yourself."

He gave her a bad-boy grin. "I want to taste the one you've already nibbled."

Blushing, Gabrielle put the sushi up to his mouth.

As he ate the California roll from the chopsticks, his eyes intently roved her beautiful face. "I agree. It is…" He started to say something about tasting her but managed not to, reminding himself to keep taking it slow with her.

The couple chatted away between bites. She had asked Cameron to tell her about Montego Bay, and he was only too happy to oblige her. He liked that she was such a good listener and that she seemed so eager to learn about the islands on the ship's itinerary.

He told her about Doctor's Cave Beach Club, nestled between the Marine Park and the Hip Strip. The translucent water on that beach in Montego Bay was known for its mineral content and its clean, inviting white sand beaches.

"Does the name have anything to do with medicine?"

"Nothing whatsoever. We can go there if you'd like, depending on how much time I get. But we'll only get to take in a couple of tourist attractions. I can't stray far."

She grabbed hold of his hand. "I know that, Cameron, and I'm glad that you're willing to do this for me. You're so knowledgeable about the islands. I couldn't ask for a better guide."

"We can always take a cruise during our five weeks off. How does that sound?"

"Nice. You love the sea, don't you? Do you plan to go back into private practice when you retire from the cruise lines?"

"I'm a sailor at heart. As doctors, we're so limited in what we can do at sea, but there are just as many stranglehold issues in private practice. I have a few ideas, but I'm always pondering my future. What about you?"

"I try to take it one day at a time. It was a big deal for me to sign on for five months, but there is an escape clause in my contract. I made sure to have it because I didn't know if I could stay on the water for five months. But I love it so far."

"It can get old, Gabby. Believe me, it can. There is a dark side to sailing. When a crewmember or a passenger leaps overboard that's hard to deal with mentally. No amount of medicine or doctoring can save them."

Her eyes grew wide. "Has that happened on your watch?"

"Twice. Both times it was crewmembers. But the news of what happens on other ships in the fleet gets around. It happens too often in my opinion."

He looked so disturbed that she leaned over and kissed him, hoping to console him. "I'm really sorry about those losses, Cameron."

"It's just the reality. The profession we're in deals with death and sorrow on a regular basis, even though it may not be one of our patients. I didn't know either of the crewmembers."

She kissed him again. "This conversation is getting a bit morbid. Can we lighten it up? I'd rather see your beautiful smile."

He gave her a soft smile, but it didn't quite light in his eyes. "Sorry I went there. What about watching some TV? I can go get DVDs from my cabin if you don't have any."

"I have plenty of movies. Go on in the living room while I clean off the table and tidy up. Do you want anything else to drink?"

"I'll grab a bottle of water from the fridge. Let me help you stack the trays so I can set them outside for pickup."

"Thanks, Cameron."

After three hours of watching television, Gabrielle had fallen asleep. Cameron lifted her and carried her to bed, where he laid her on the side she'd slept on last night. She had lifted her head momentarily during transport then fallen off to sleep again. Recalling where she'd gotten her nightclothes from, he went over to the dresser and pulled open a drawer.

Looking at some of the sexy unmentionables she wore, he whistled softly, wondering if he'd ever get to see her in the alluring lingerie. He turned and glanced at her, hoping she had on something sexy under the beautiful white dress. As he thought about undressing her and redressing her for bed, he remembered she hadn't slept in anything sexy last night. After the bonfire they'd had to put out prematurely, Cameron figured she'd worn something conservative on purpose. Gabrielle had very interesting ways about her, which set her far apart from others.

He carefully searched for something she'd find appropriate to sleep in with a man she was wildly attracted to but wasn't making love to. How many more nights would he be able to do this? Cameron planned to handle it for as many nights as it took him to win her trust.

He wasn't thinking about guarding his heart anymore, not when it came to a woman like her. She was so different from anyone he'd known and he wanted to know everything about her. His thoughts turned to her brother for a second—Maxwell was a good man, too.

Cameron saw that he was terribly proud of his sister and that he held her in high esteem.

Standing over the bed, he removed her shoes first, which caused her to stir. He then lifted her to her back and began removing the dress. It wasn't as easy as he'd thought it would be, but he'd get it off even if it took him an hour.

Gabrielle opened her eyes and smiled playfully at him. "Let me help you out."

He checked her with a suspicious eye. "Have you been playing possum all along?"

She grinned. "Only for a couple of seconds, after you sat me up. Your touch was so tender." She carefully pulled the dress up over her head and handed it to him.

His eyes grew large at the white lace panties she wore. Once again, she was braless. He steeled himself so that he wouldn't react to her nude upper body, but it was close to impossible. "Don't do anything else. I want to dress you for bed. Wait until I hang this up in the closet, and cover up so you don't catch cold."

Gabrielle laughed at the concerned expression on his face. They were going to get into big trouble yet.

Cameron rushed right back to Gabrielle. Seated on the side of the bed, he put a black silk pajama top on her. His eyes stared into hers as he buttoned it up. He lifted one leg to help her into the pajama bottoms then he lifted the other. "Lift yourself so I can finish pulling them on."

Gabrielle felt giddy. "Gladly! I like having you as my personal valet."

Since Cameron had said he didn't sleep in pajamas, she decided to take the pleasure of undressing him down to his briefs. Looking straight into his eyes, she began unbuttoning his shirt. Then she pushed it off his shoulders and ran her fingers through his thick chest hair. She threw her arms around his neck then pushed him back on the bed and kissed him passionately.

Lifting her head, Gabrielle gently teased his bottom lip with her fingernails. "We're playing with fire, Dr. Quinn. I hope neither of us gets burned."

"No one is getting burned. Now please finish what you started, Dr. Grinage."

She gave him one of her naughty looks. "My pleasure."

Chapter 10

Cameron settled down beside Gabrielle in bed and laid his head on her stomach. Her fingertips tenderly massaged his scalp. As she tenderly gripped the rich texture of his hair, tugging gently, his entire body shivered. Goose bumps and heat clashed together like rivals.

It was becoming very obvious to him that she didn't know how much power she held over him. It was as if she hadn't felt his reaction to her. He believed she had a world of confidence in herself, but he felt as though she hadn't fully regained any conviction in trusting romantic relationships. Vulnerability screamed out from inside her, as loud as a siren.

His thoughts took him to the day she'd come over to the table to meet him during orientation. Her picture and bio had already wowed him weeks before. Cameron had found himself totally fascinated by her as she'd walked over to get into line. He'd never been stunned off his feet while sitting down, not in the presence of any woman. It had amazed him even then that he'd thought he'd do just about anything for her. All she'd have to do was ask.

Gabrielle leaned down and blew into his ear. "Why're you so quiet?"

Cameron turned over and placed the back of his head on her lap. His eyes slowly captured hers. "I'm not. My thoughts of you are louder than my voice."

With his eyes riveted on her, she knew he saw how deeply she was moved by his unique comment. She had an idea of what he'd meant, but she wanted to hear it from him. "Do you mind explaining that?"

"It's just that I can't stop thinking about you, though I'm right here by your side."

"Can you tell me what you're thinking? Is it good or bad?"

"It's neither. I'm just making observations in my head."

"Cameron, you're driving me crazy."

He sat up. "By thinking?"

"By not telling me what you're thinking," she said in an exasperated tone.

"Do you tell me everything you're thinking?" He wasn't surprised by her haughty voice. He'd heard it in the clinic when she'd confronted him about announcing their relationship.

Gritting her teeth, she glared at him. "This isn't funny."

"I don't hear anyone laughing, Gabby." Maybe this needed to happen, he thought. Perhaps he could get through to her if he could manage to break through the iceberg she'd freeze into when her insecurities hit.

Cameron stiffened as Gabrielle tried to move off the bed. "Where are you off to in such a hurry?"

She crossed her arms. "You're the one who's off to somewhere, commander. I'm home."

He smirked. "Are you asking or telling me to leave? But before you answer that, are you the same person who said you weren't a little girl?"

She didn't like his tone. "Why are you asking me that now?"

"Because you're acting like a child, Gabby. And for no reason."

Gabrielle turned her head away from Cameron. She felt terrible but didn't know how to put on the brakes to the crazy roller-coaster ride they were on.

"Does the second in command give permission for the commander to leave?"

"You're the commander," she shot back curtly.

He busted up laughing. "Military service would've done your bad attitude some good. Now you got me acting childish, just like you."

Gabrielle turned over and pulled a face at him. "How's that for childish?"

"How's this for manly? I'm the man, your man."

Cameron brought her head close to his. His lips burned a fiery path onto hers until he blazed a wild-fire against her mouth. As she tried to push him away, he kissed her more passionately. Pinning her arms back to stop her flailing, he took full advantage of the lips he loved to taste and the woman he constantly craved. His tongue pushed its way past her clenched teeth and into her mouth. As he looped his tongue around hers, he kissed her deeper and deeper, hoping she'd give in to his endless desire for her.

Unable to put up any more resistance, Gabrielle gave him what he wanted and what she couldn't do without for another second. She kissed him back fiercely, hungrily, ravishing his mouth with hot, moist kisses. As he let go of her hands to wrap her tightly in his arms, she pushed her hand between them and toyed with the hair on his chest. She tweaked his hardened nipples between her two fingertips and heard his moans coming from deep within.

He gently tilted her head. Wanting to capture her entire being, he kissed her neck and throat, delighted by the sweet taste of her soft, creamy skin. Perfume still lingered on her and he became enraptured by the scent of her heavenly fragrance.

"If I tell you I'm sorry, will you forgive me?" Gabrielle whispered against his lips.

"Try me."

"I'm sorry. I was a brat. Insecurities come at me unexpectedly, and I rarely fail to react."

He cupped her face. "You don't have to be insecure around me. I'm a real man, baby, an extremely good one. I don't do to people what I don't want done to me."

"I was taught that and so were most people, but not everyone understands it."

He held her away from him and his eyes locked with hers. "That's your problem. You confuse me with other men. I only know how to be me, the best me I can be. I'm no one else."

"I am confused a good bit of the time, but I know you're a wonderful man. Still, I can't help being scared. You're the first man I've allowed in, and I want to be okay. Help me."

Leaning his head against hers, he kissed her tenderly.

"I'm here, and only you can make me go away. I don't want to go, Gabby. I want to stay."

She kissed his eyelids. "Then stay. Don't let me send you away."

He grinned. "Did you really think I'd leave you alone in the mood you were in?"

"Honestly?" She shrugged. "I wasn't sure, but I want to be sure about you."

"A real man stays to help his lady through her struggles."

She laughed softly. "Don't pinch me if this is a dream."

He put her hand up to his lips and kissed her fingertips. "I can be your dream man if you want, but I'm always for real."

Cameron's on-call cell went off the moment the sweet words left his mouth. "We both know what that means. Looks like changing my schedule didn't help."

He answered the cell phone and listened intently to what was said. "Get Philip to meet me there. I'm on my way."

Cameron hung up and stood quickly. "This one may take a while. Do you want me to come back?"

"Let's decide when you're finished. Is there something I can do to help?"

Nearly dressed, he leaned down and kissed her. "I'll call if I need more help, but you're not on call. Phillip is."

Cameron went to the door but came back and kissed Gabrielle three times before he had no choice but to leave. The emergency was in a cabin on the other side of the ship.

Gabrielle had mixed emotions about Cameron leaving. On one hand, she'd miss him, but on the other hand, it'd keep them out of trouble awhile longer. Things had heated up again and she wasn't sure how much longer her body could deny this crazy need for him.

There had been no word from Cameron since he'd kissed her goodbye after the emergency call. She felt out of sorts. She'd been pacing her cabin back and forth, in between the living room and bedroom alcove, and up and down the hallway leading to the front door. She looked at the clock for the umpteenth time. This was the longest emergency since she'd come aboard, and none of the other staff had any information on it.

Where was Cameron? Was he okay? Why hadn't he called to give her an update? He more than likely had his hands full. She assured herself that Cameron must be unable to call, otherwise she would've heard from him.

Gabrielle opened the balcony door and went outside. The warm breeze engulfed her, and she leaned against the railing and watched the cresting waves. The sea wasn't as calm as it had been earlier, but there was still no danger. She made it a point to keep up with the weather watch on the TV, where they gave updates on conditions every half hour. At least they weren't in hurricane season—she'd lived under hurricane watches her entire life.

Gabrielle sat down on the chaise lounge and tried to decide what she could do to keep busy. She'd already watched more television than she normally did, but just sitting around her cabin was driving her crazy. In the next instant she decided to change into running gear and jog on the uppermost deck of the ship.

Jumping up from the chaise, she went back inside

and headed straight to the dresser drawer, where she kept her jogging attire. She pulled out a pair of New Balance sneakers, which were comfortable to run in. She dressed in sleek black and gray spandex pants, a T-shirt and a hooded jacket. Once she tied her hair back with a scarf she was ready to go.

She picked up her key card from the table and headed out the front door. Before leaving, she stepped back inside and left the hall light on. She'd come in to a darkened place too many times.

Out the door now, she started out with an even stride and planned to break into a full jog once she got up on the track. Instead of taking the elevators to the top deck, she ran into the stairwell and took the first of five flights. She realized she'd forgotten her personal cell phone and thought about going back for it, but decided she didn't need it.

Coming through the stairwell doors on the top deck, she felt good enough to run around the track until she'd clocked a couple of miles. A relaxing soak in the on-deck Jacuzzi after would keep her muscles from tightening up and further relax her and prep her for a good night's sleep. She kept swimwear in a spa locker she had rented.

"Hey, Gabrielle."

Gabrielle turned around and saw Marjorie and Tristan jogging right behind her. Instead of running back to them, she slowed her pace so they'd catch up with her.

"Where's the commander?" Tristan asked.

Keeping up a good jogging pace, Gabrielle frowned. "He was on an emergency, but he's been gone a long time. Am I worrying needlessly?"

"No reason to worry." Marjorie assured her. "We have emergencies on every cruise, some worse than others, but the emergency crew has always managed to get things under control."

"What are you and Tristan doing after jogging?"

"We're hanging out in the casino for a while. Want to join us?"

"Thanks, I may do that. I want to soak in the Jacuzzi for a half hour or so, then I can go back to the cabin and get dressed."

Marjorie looked at her watch. "What about meeting us there at seven?"

"I'll see. If I don't get there at seven, it'll be soon after. Do you think I should call Cameron if he doesn't call me?"

"No, you shouldn't. Sometimes emergencies are complicated, and you can trust him to call you when he's free. He told Tristan and me that he's got it bad for you."

Gabrielle's eyes widened. "Was he serious or joking around?"

"My friend, he was as serious as I've ever seen him. You feel like that about him?"

"I must admit that I do. Cameron is special, and I believe in him."

"He's the man to believe in. I've known him for a while, and you're the only woman he's shown any interest in since I've been here. He rarely socialized around the ship until you came."

Gabrielle sighed. "He's pretty much told me that too. I'm so into him. Still, I get scared. He promised to help me through the troubled waters."

"Lean on him, and he'll hold you up until you can

stand on your own two feet." As Marjorie pulled Gabrielle out of the way of other joggers, they slowed their pace. "I have to tell you something. I don't know if Cameron knows this or not, but I heard from the ship's grapevine that Amanda Abraham is allegedly aboard this ship."

Gabrielle was stunned. "That *is* some news. Do you think she's his emergency?"

"Don't take yourself there. If he knew she was here, he would've told you. I believe that wholeheartedly. Cameron wouldn't sneak around behind your back."

Gabrielle felt like her skin had turned ashy. Fear was tearing away at her resolve. "Look, I'm skipping the Jacuzzi soak and getting back to my cabin in case he needs me. If I don't show at the casino, it's because he and I are together."

Marjorie nodded. "Go with Cameron, Gabrielle. Put every ounce of your trust in him."

Gabrielle rushed into her cabin and stripped away her clothing as she made it to her bed. The red light on the phone wasn't flashing, which meant she had no messages. She planned to take Marjorie's advice and wait for Cameron to call her. It was hours since she'd last seen him. When he'd asked her if she'd wanted him to come back, why couldn't she have just given him an honest response? Of course she wanted him to come back.

"Are you with Amanda, Cameron? I hope that you don't even know she's here. And I hope it's nothing more than a silly rumor."

She knew she couldn't hear the phone in the shower but she had to bathe. She was sweaty from running, and the water from the shower would mingle with her tears and help disguise them.

There still was no message from Cameron when she came out of the shower, feeling refreshed. Gabrielle sat down on the bed and turned on her brand-new Apple computer then searched for the name Amanda Abraham, M.D. Getting a look at Cameron's last love interest was either going to satisfy her curiosity or make her wish she hadn't dared to make this silly search.

She knew Amanda was Cameron's past, just as Jordan was hers. Cameron had said that to her so many times, but here she was digging up the past.

"Oh, my goodness," Gabrielle gasped, staring wide-eyed at Cameron's ex-girlfriend. She was an exotic beauty and appeared to be a mix of Asian and African-American. Her dark, almond-shaped eyes were expressively beautiful; gorgeous, long black hair framed her oval face like a satin curtain. Gabrielle speed-read Amanda's bio and educational and professional standings. "Impressive."

Feeling even more dismayed than before, Gabrielle closed the site and shut down her laptop.

She gasped at the sudden knock on her door. Her hands trembled as she put them up to her mouth. She walked into the hallway, not sure she wanted it to be Cameron. Her reaction had more than likely come out of guilt over looking into Amanda's history. She'd never reacted that way when a knock came of the door.

There was another knock and she flinched. She turned back to her bed, realizing she was in no state to see anyone right then. Several minutes later, all was quiet outside her door.

If his ex-girlfriend was on this cruise, Gabrielle didn't know if she could stand it if Cameron wanted to see her again. It would hurt like hell. She wondered if the boyfriend Amanda had gone back to, the one she'd chosen over Cameron, was sailing with her. That would be an interesting mix, but it'd also mean they were still together. She smiled at the thought.

She laid down on her bed, and tears spilled from her eyes. Fear shook her very foundation. Cameron had said he was a real man, the one who would stay when his lady struggled.

What if his ex-lady was struggling and she needed him to stay and help her out? Would he consider helping her through it?

You're being such a fool, Gabrielle. You don't have to fight for Cameron because he's fighting for you and him. He's also fighting for you to sever the past. You're about to botch this relationship big time. And you don't even know if Amanda's really on this ship.

Still, Gabrielle wasn't quite ready to face him. Not in this chaotic state. Her nerves were raw, and there was no way she could hide her vulnerabilities from him. He would pick up on her fear and insecurities immediately. One look into her eyes would reveal to him that she was lost.

Gabrielle got up from the bed in a hurry and ran into the bathroom, where she stripped out of her robe and hung it. She zoomed through the few steps back to the bedroom and got dressed in haste, then put on her makeup quicker than ever before. Then she grabbed an oversized white patent-leather bag and key card and left her suite. She couldn't get out of her cabin fast enough. Being with other people would hopefully fill her mind with more pleasant things. Thinking about Cameron constantly wasn't helping her to keep her mind off his past love.

If they'd somehow gotten together, she'd die of a broken heart the moment she found out.

Gabrielle gracefully strolled into the casino, and the ringing bells and excited yelps instantly put her in a totally different mind-set. She checked around for Marjorie. Unable to find her, she continued to stroll through the room.

"Hey, beautiful, what are you doing alone?" asked a hunky older gentleman with massive muscles. "You can hang out with me. I can teach you how to win big at the poker table."

She smiled softly. "I'm meeting friends. Thanks for the offer."

"Enjoy yourself, sweet cheeks," he said, giving her a big, toothy grin before walking off.

Gabrielle chuckled inwardly, wondering what she'd done to deserve the icky nickname.

A colorful machine caught Gabrielle's eye. It had a bunch of sevens decorated in red, white and blue stars and stripes. She looked around, as though she was checking out who was in the vicinity, then she plopped down on the stool. She pulled a hundred-dollar bill from her purse, and stared at it.

Gabrielle couldn't remember a thing Cameron had told her about how these games were played. She looked around again. The muscled guy just happened to pass by again, and she summoned him with a wave of her hand. "Can you help me?"

"Of course I can. What you need? By the way, I'm Barry Cohen. What's your name?"

"I'm Gabrielle Grinage, and I need a real quick lesson in understanding how this slot machine works."

"If you're not going to play all the pay-lines, it could turn out to be a waste of time. I suggest you pay all three lines. That's seventy-five cents a pop."

Barry then told Gabrielle she could pull the arm down or just press in two small buttons to make one or two bets. The large button was for betting all pay-lines.

"Go ahead and give it a whirl. I'll stay here to see if you got it."

She held up the hundred-dollar bill. "If I put this in there, do I have to use it all?"

"When you want to stop, just push the payout button."

"Thanks. You were a big help."

"Glad to oblige. You remind me of my beautiful daughter. She's about your age and is just as pretty as you are. There's a lucky man out there somewhere for both of you." He threw up his hand and gave her a cheery farewell.

Gabrielle was a fast learner, though she wished she had a ten or twenty to start out with. But this was a one-time deal, so she didn't let it worry her. "Win or lose," she said, chuckling.

She played all three pay-lines. The screen told her how much money she'd lose or win. Three identical sevens came up draped in fancy sequined stars and stripes. Each seven stopped on the pay-line, and she knew she'd won but she had no idea how much. Then the bells started ringing, rapidly racking up her winnings.

A woman came over to her and smiled. "You just

won big. Congratulations! You're looking at eighteen hundred greenbacks."

Gabrielle was astounded. "You're kidding. Eighteen hundred dollars?"

"Exactly right. If I were you, I'd take my money and fly this coop, sugar."

"I think I'll take your advice." Gabrielle noticed a light red ball on top of the machine. "What does that mean?"

"Take your card over to the cage and someone will help you get your money loaded."

"Thank you. You've been helpful." Gabrielle knew exactly what to do with the winnings. She was the acting president of the Grinage Foundation, a doctor/student organization her parents had founded that helped doctors mentor underprivileged teen girls and boys who wanted to go into medicine. Her winnings would be deposited into the Grinage Scholarship Fund.

Marjorie and Tristan ran up behind Gabrielle. "Where've you been? I thought you weren't coming or got lost."

Gabrielle beamed at her friend and her handsome dude. "What I got is a windfall. I won eighteen hundred dollars on a slot machine."

"You did what?" Marjorie screeched. "That's quite a haul for a nongambler."

"I don't have it in my hands yet. I need to take my card to the cage to cash out."

"Congratulations," Tristan said, kissing her cheek. "That's a huge win."

"Sorry, but I only did a quick look for you when I first got here, then a machine summoned me with its glitzy stars and stripes. I love all things patriotic. Sucker, huh?"

Tristan and Marjorie laughed.

"Now that we found you, let's continue introducing you to this ship. Interested in going up on deck and checking out the Sounds of Calypso? They're an excellent band," Marjorie said. "Let's get you cashed out first."

"I'm all in. Let's get this party started."

But will it really be a party without my boyfriend? He's still missing in action, and I have no choice but to wait.

Tristan ushered the women out of the casino and they boarded a glass elevator to take them topside, where anything crazy and wild could happen—and most always did.

As soon as they came on deck they could hear the blaring, come-hither, bone-stirring music. Taking Tristan and Gabrielle by the hand, Marjorie moved them closer to the crowd of dancers, though people were spinning and gyrating all over the place. Even the people in the pool were rocking wildly to the music.

Gabrielle suddenly stopped in her tracks. "There he is." Her heart trembled as she saw none other than Amanda Abraham come up behind Cameron and tap him on the shoulder. He turned around to face her. Now his back was to Gabrielle and she couldn't see his expression. Was he smiling or frowning, happy or upset? They walked off together, and she figured smiling and happy had won the moment.

Gabrielle's heart ached terribly. Fighting back her tears, she conceded defeat. Amanda was back and on board, and all the garbage Cameron had fed her was just that, garbage. What about all the beautiful things he'd said to her before the emergency? Was there even a real emergency or was Amanda his emergency?

Gabrielle walked over to Marjorie and Tristan. "I have to go."

Marjorie's eyes searched her face. "Did you hear from Cameron?"

Gabrielle nodded. "I did, loud and clear. I'll see you at work tomorrow." Before Marjorie could talk her into staying, Gabrielle took off running toward one of the exit doors.

Tears fell as Gabrielle took the stairwell to try to avoid seeing anyone from the crew, especially Cameron and his past love. But maybe she was no longer in the past. It killed her to know that Amanda's appearance on board wasn't a rumor but the truth.

Ten minutes later, at the door of her cabin, Gabrielle's fingers shook badly as she inserted the key card. She headed straight for the kitchen, where she opened the fridge and retrieved a cold bottle of water. If she was a drinker, she would've mixed up a stiff cocktail to help her forget the pain and give her courage to face the man she was in love with. She went out on the balcony, then rethought her choice. What if Cameron and Amanda ended up on his balcony?

She tore back inside and plopped down on the sofa.

Even though she knew it wasn't going to ring, Gabrielle still stared hard at the phone. Cameron was otherwise engaged, and her name probably hadn't crossed his mind since he'd left. She sat up straight. She decided it was time to analyze their entire relationship, or what she thought was a relationship, an exclusive one.

Once again, combining love and labor had been the culprit. She had been so adamant about not getting involved in another love affair with a coworker but then she'd thrown caution to the wind. That was why all this was happening.

Gabrielle felt like she had egg on her face again. She hadn't paid attention to her first impression of Jordan and she'd paid a high price. Then she'd repeated the same gigantic mistake by getting involved with Cameron when she knew it could never work. She had willfully set herself up for the worst fall of all. He wasn't just another doctor; he was her commander, her boss. But unlike Jordan, Gabrielle liked Cameron tremendously, and she was also in love with him.

"It's over. I'm not giving this another thought. There's nothing he can say to make me change my mind. Lust, labor and love are deadly combinations." Even as the words left her mouth, her uncontrollable tears flowed.

The phone rang and Gabrielle ignored it. If it was Cameron, and she was sure it was by her heart's reaction, she was no longer available to him. Amanda had obviously come first with him, even when he knew she was waiting to hear from him.

There was nothing for her and Cameron to talk about outside of work. Luckily, she also had a way out of her five-month commitment. She'd get the hell off this ship and request to be resigned to another cruise liner in the same fleet. A reassignment was possible before the five months were actually up, she considered. A move would be best for everyone.

Chapter 11

Loud pounding on her cabin door woke Gabrielle from a fitful sleep. She turned over on her back and laid her head flat onto the pillow. Her phone had been blowing up all evening, and now the door was being bombarded. She didn't have to guess who was out there. No one but Cameron Quinn could be responsible for all this god-forsaken chaos.

She heard a keycard be inserted into the cabin door, and she sat straight up in bed. Fear streaked through her eyes as she crept out of bed and went over to the closet, where she armed herself with a heavy metal tennis racket. Then she took a spray bottle of mace out of a drawer. She moved into the center of the bed and sat cross-legged, surveying the entire cabin, ready for whoever had plans of invading her personal space. She heard whispering, and she leaned forward to try to hear what was said.

Lights flooded the cabin, starling her something fierce.

"Dr. Grinage, it's security. Are you okay? I'm coming into the living area. Shout out to me if you're okay and I'll back off."

"I'm okay. Sorry for the inconvenience. Did you come because there's been suspicious activity in the area?"

"We had calls from several people who were concerned. I'm leaving now, but Dr. Quinn wants to check you out to make sure you're okay physically. Sorry for disturbing you."

Gabrielle went into a panic, but she wasn't surprised by Cameron's tactics. He was a man who liked to be heard. But he wasn't callous, no matter what a monster she'd made him out to be in her mind.

Cameron walked into the alcove and just stood there looking at her. He wasn't wearing a happy expression. His eyes narrowed and raked her over the hot coals. "Why?"

She shrugged with nonchalance. "Why what?"

He moved over to the bed and sat on the side of the mattress. "Don't play coy with me. Why have you ignored my hundreds of calls?"

She jutted her chin in an act of defiance. "I was too busy pondering my past, too tied up wallowing in it. You were right—I have no future. I now accept your observations on my life."

His brow wrinkled. "Sarcasm doesn't become you. When I left you, we were happy and in love."

She threw out her hands. "Just goes to show how quickly things change. I'm still happy but not in love. My dreadful past won't let me love ever again."

"So we're back to your past. You do love to revisit ashes."

She shot him an angry glance of intolerance. "That's me. Ashes to ashes, dust to dust, the state of my non-existent love life."

He looked troubled. "We need to have a serious talk, Gabrielle." Instead of asking her to get up, he took off his shoes and laid down, turning on his side. He'd made it a point to keep out of striking distance, and she knew she looked like she wanted to hit something.

Her heart thudded hard against her ribs. She didn't like the serious expression he wore and she didn't know what in the world might come out of his mouth. But she was curious enough to sit there and listen.

He took her hand. "Earlier I told you I was thinking about you, and I'm concerned about a few things. One of the things is your opt-out contract clause, though I understand it. Where do you see yourself in the next few years? What are your goals for practicing medicine after this sea stint?"

Gabrielle looked perplexed. "What does this have to do with anything?"

"It has everything to do with us, Gabrielle. Please answer my questions."

Her insides shook like Jell-O. "This may surprise you, but I want to someday become a wife and mother. My parents did all right with a houseful of kids and full-time careers. Before age forty, I'd like to have a baby or two. What about you? Can you answer the same questions?"

"I can honestly say I'd never thought about being a father. That is, until I met you." Moisture shone bright in his eyes. "I can see you as the mother of my children.

I'd want a daughter to look just like you and a son in my image. It's premature, but it's not just a fantasy. Please hear me out, Gabrielle. Something happened today that accelerated my thoughts.

"Your insecurities worry me more than anything else in our relationship. Despite your saucy replies, if you don't find a way to cut ties with your past, your future is grim."

"I'm well aware of that, and this isn't the first time you've said it. It's like a running diatribe. Have *you* completely cut ties with your past?" Her eyes pierced into his. The answer to this question would tell her a lot.

"Seeing how you reacted so haughtily to me got me thinking about what a future with you would really be like. I personally think you've still been reacting to Jordan. I figured you weren't going to have a future with love as long as the hurt he caused is around. And it sickened me that I'd also be excluded from your future."

She was worried about what this heart-to-heart meant. "Why are we having this conversation now? Is that what you were so thoughtful about when I went into a major funk?"

He desperately wanted to touch her but he knew she wouldn't want him to. "Our relationship is so new, but I want it to grow and grow and never get old. I love the sea, as you know. But I can't see cruising around the world, practicing medicine, while a wife waits at home for my ship to come in. That wouldn't be a life for a spouse and certainly not for children. I want to be a deeply involved dad and a super-supportive husband when the time comes."

Gabrielle shrugged. "I don't see where you're going

with this. We're nowhere in the ballpark of marriage and kids. We're just getting to know each other."

"Stop kidding yourself, Gabby. We're soul mates. No genius had to tell me that. And if you don't recall, let me say it again. I'm a man who knows exactly what he wants."

Gabrielle sighed. "I recall."

"I know it's hard to put it all out there at once. What I want to know is if you can hang in there with me. I know I can hang with you. If I know your goals, and what you want from life, and love, it'll help me considerably with this crisis I've suddenly found myself in."

"I'm willing to take everything I can get out of life and love...and not take it lightly," she replied. "But not only that, I plan to give back. I want a great partnership filled with love, life and with a man who loves me." She still didn't understand the urgency in this talk, but obviously there were things he wanted to know from her. Something had happened to him and it had jolted him badly.

"What was your first reaction to me? Did flashing warning signs go off in your head like they did with Jordan?"

Her heart began to thump wildly. "I had a totally different reaction to you, but I don't want to get into it. Suffice to say, I immediately thought you seemed kind and compassionate."

Cameron grinned. "You were spot-on with that. Is there anything that you want to do professionally or personally that you haven't mentioned yet?"

Gabrielle took a minute to think about his question. "There is one goal I burn white hot for. I'd love to join Doctors Without Borders before I go have babies. It's been a lifelong dream. And I also want to continue growing my parents' scholarship fund and keep mentoring underprivileged kids who want to become doctors."

Cameron's eyes lit up like fireworks at midnight. "Joining Doctors without Borders is my main goal for when I settle on dry land." He looked at her as though he couldn't believe his goals and hers had matched up so perfectly. But why not? They were a perfect match in every other area.

"You've given me the help I needed. I think we belong together for as long as we want to give ourselves to each other. And I don't give myself lightly, Gabby."

"Neither do I," she said tearfully.

He pulled her to him, but she pushed him away.

Gabrielle's tears spilled over. "Since we're having a heart-to-heart, I need to unburden the heavy load that's on my heart. I saw Amanda come up behind you on deck and tap you on the shoulder. What was your reaction when you saw her?"

Cameron was surprised that Gabrielle had seen him and Amanda. But what surprised him more was how she knew it was Amanda.

"How do you know what Amanda looks like?"

"Google. I only looked up her name after I'd heard she was aboard the ship."

He was relieved, glad that Gabrielle hadn't looked her up simply because she'd had a desire to see what Amanda looked like. It wasn't like her to do it for any other reason. But regardless, Amanda had nothing on Gabrielle in looks, heart, spirit and personality.

"I'll answer your question. I didn't have a reaction, not even irritation. She has no power over me, never really did. I forgave her long ago. I did it for me."

Gabrielle looked stumped. "What do you mean by that?"

"Forgiveness is not for the person we need to forgive. It's for the person who needs to forgive. Was I surprised by my reaction to her? I was, but when I cut ties with her, they were cut forever. I never looked back, because I already knew what I'd find behind me."

"Interesting. Forgiveness is important, and I learned that the hard way." She blew out a gust of air. "I...I didn't know what to think. You were gone for so long. I kept waiting for you here in the cabin, but when you never came back, I went out for a while with Marjorie and Tristan. And then I saw you with Amanda."

"I did come back, several times, after I repeatedly called the cabin and your cell. I also couldn't reach Marjorie or Tristan. Then I thought you might be ill, so I alerted security. If I hadn't told everyone about us, I wouldn't have been allowed in here with security. You're also my second in command."

She looked ashamed. "The ringers on both phones were turned off. Because you'd been gone for hours, I assumed you'd been with Amanda all that time. I convinced myself she was your emergency."

Cameron looked pained. "Gabrielle, Gabrielle, have I not shown you my true feelings? Have I not tried to become your present and help you lose your past? I was with you when my on-call cell went off." Cameron put his head down momentarily. "How could you question my medical and moral ethics? I'd never tell you there was an emergency as a ruse to see another woman."

"Why is Amanda aboard the ship?"

He shrugged his shoulders. "No clue. When I walked away from her, I heard her yell 'I'm getting a divorce.' I never so much as looked back. I didn't even know she'd gotten married. That's how much I've concerned myself with her." Without hesitation he took Gabrielle's mouth in a blistering kiss.

Gabrielle gasped and she inhaled his familiar scent. As tears rolled from her eyes, she lifted up his head and looked into his eyes. "I lost you on deck, Cameron. I thought you saw me and didn't care."

He kissed her again, and it was clear he didn't want to talk. Kissing her and touching her tenderly was the only thing on his mind. The emergency had been an awful one, and he needed the comforting arms of the woman he was rapidly becoming addicted to. He kissed her again and again and again, devouring her mouth with his, touching and tasting her until he felt her very essence.

Cameron held her slightly away from him. "Gabrielle, I need you. Please, I have to be with you. I missed you." Tears filled his eyes.

"I missed you, too, every minute you were gone."

"I need to shower and change clothes. Will you shower with me? I don't want us apart for a fraction of a second."

"I guess we'll go to your cabin since you have to change clothes. I'll go with you."

He put his arm around her shoulders, a sudden sadness drowning in his eyes. "Both cabins are *ours*. I want you with me, Gabrielle."

She kissed his forehead. "I can't deny you anything I'm capable of giving. I'm sorry I doubted you yet again."

Gabrielle saw the sadness in Cameron's eyes. She knew something heavy was going on with him. Perhaps the emergency had been a bad one, but was something more than that happening with him? Knowing where her mind wanted to go, she redirected her thoughts. No matter what Cameron needed from her, she had it to give. If she didn't have it in her, she'd find it in a hurry even if she had to pull it out of thin air. Cameron's needs were her needs, and he'd already proved to her that her needs were his.

Gabrielle ran her fingers through his hair. "Do you want to talk about your medical emergency?"

He wrinkled his nose. "You can hear it during our briefing tomorrow. Is that okay?"

"Whatever you're comfortable with, Commander."

Suddenly, Cameron broke down crying. "Our team lost a patient today. Phillip and I did everything in our power to save the passenger."

Gabrielle held Cameron's head against her breasts, stroking his back and rubbing his arms. "I'm so sorry." Tears sprang to her eyes. "I can only imagine how you feel. I'm sure you and the entire team did all you could. The outcome is not always in our hands."

A seventy-year-old male had suffered a massive heart attack. He'd been airlifted in an emergency helicopter to the nearest hospital after the ship's medical team had done all they could do to stabilize him. Cameron told Gabrielle that several hours later, rescue services radioed back, informing the ship's medical team that the man had succumbed before he was wheeled into the E.R.

They held each other quietly for several minutes. Finally, Cameron rose so they could go shower.

He opened his cabin and allowed her to precede him, then immediately began undressing. Once he was naked, he lifted her from the sofa and stood her on her feet. Quicker than he'd undressed, he had her stripped nude. Taking her hand, he led her into the bathroom, where they stepped into the glass shower, turned on the water and closed the door.

Cameron removed the shower gel from the caddy and squirted it all over her body. He handed the gel to her, telling her to lather him up. Although Gabrielle felt a little timid, she lathered him up. Then he stayed Gabrielle's hand. "You took care of me and it's my turn to do you."

Gabrielle laughed heartily. "*Do me.* You're going to *do me* with shower gel?"

Cameron grinned devilishly. "You tell me, after we're through."

Wanting to leave no part of her unattended, he massaged the gel over her entire body, slipping his hands between her legs and over her thighs to lather up her sensitive areas. He didn't linger there long, because he planned to revisit the very core of her sensuality.

Wide, swirling motions with his teasing hands took care of soaping her firm buttocks. Carefully pressing her back against the cool glass, he used the tip of his fingers to spread suds on her neck and throat. He licked his lips, then drew large circles in gel around her beautiful breasts and outlined her nipples with smaller gel rings. He dipped his head and drew a taut nipple into his mouth, letting his tongue and teeth work her into a squirming frenzy.

The blush on her face and skin had him turned on. It was time for them to wash off, but he had a unique method in mind for her. She wasn't ready to make wild passionate love to him, but that didn't mean he couldn't utterly satisfy her natural desires and make her scream for more. After dialing the shower head to a warm, pulsating spray, Cameron gave it to her to rinse him off.

Gabrielle had been shivering, but Cameron's hands had turned up her body heat. As she ran water over his flesh, pleasure showed on his face.

Gabrielle passed the shower head back to him.

Pulling her to him, he kissed her passionately. "Ready for me to do you, babe?"

All she could do was smile.

Taking his time, he rinsed the upper portion of her body. As the clean water ran down her breasts, he caught it with his mouth, kissing her, without spitting out the water. Dropping to his knees, he positioned his head right below the core of her. He ran more water into his mouth from the shower head, then he leaned down and rinsed her intimate core with the water inside his mouth. With one hand clamped firmly around her leg, he rinsed her off again, his tongue getting in on the action to lap the moisture away.

As he noticed her legs shaking and becoming unstable, he sat down on the shower floor and brought her down onto his lap. He kissed her breathlessly, and his hands explored every inch of the tender flesh surrounding the areas of her most intimate self.

Inserting one finger into her core, he tenderly went to work on the one place he craved. He wanted to fully satisfy Gabrielle without actually making love to her. There were countless ways to bring her sexual gratification, but none of that was as important as bringing contentment to her soul. It was his job to make sure he didn't do anything to inflict pain on her heart and spirit. She needed his love and support.

Cameron felt the riotous explosion the moment it

erupted inside her. Gathering her trembling body closer to his, he held her tightly, whispering her name softly. As she screamed out his name, time and time again, he covered her mouth with his and silenced her.

Cameron looked into Gabrielle's eyes. "I love you, Gabby."

"I love you, too." A tear escaped the corner of her eye.

"Sad tears or happy ones?" Cameron asked, gently kissing it away.

"Very happy ones."

Cameron carried Gabrielle out of the shower and wrapped her up in one of his thick terry robes. He brought her into the bedroom and settled her on his bed. "Can I make you some hot tea?"

Gabrielle looked up at him with an unreadable expression in her eyes. She reached her hand out to him. "You said you didn't want us apart, not for a second. Has that changed?"

"Nothing has changed." Slipping into bed with her, he drew Gabrielle into his arms, and held her tight. "Are you okay?"

She swallowed hard. "That's never happened to me before."

He looked puzzled. "What's never happened?"

"The way you charmed, seduced then conquered me in the shower. I surrendered all. I've never felt anything like it in my life, never had skyrockets shooting off inside my body. Have I been missing something?"

"You've been missing me, baby. What I did to you and with you was also a first for me. I'm always thinking of ways to love and satisfy you, original ways. Nothing I've done in the past is good enough for you. That's what makes you so special—you make a man want to try something new and to continuously perfect the way I treat you. All I want is to bring you pleasure, designed solely for you. You bring that need out in me, girl."

"I can't tell you all the things you bring out in me. I'm ready to let go of the past, Cameron. I almost lost you by letting the past guide my thoughts and actions."

Cameron kissed her sweetly. "At the end of these five months, we can assess our relationship if you want. But I'm already positive about our future as one."

"I like your plan. In the meantime, we'll stick together like glue."

Gabrielle sat up in bed and removed the robe. "I've had my first wild ride on the waves of your passion, and now I'm hungry for all night long."

Finally ready for all of him, she straddled Cameron and slowly took him inside her, looking into his eyes all the while. As he sat up to bring them even closer together, she gasped wantonly. Their lips met in a fiery kiss and she lost herself in the intimacy of their bodies entwined together. She couldn't get enough of him, and she rocked her hips back and forth and moaned at the rewarding pleasures he offered back.

Cameron was prepared to steer the ship for as long as she wanted to ride the waves. He rolled her on her back without losing the intimate connection. She was hot and he hoped she never cooled down with him. He was so sure of what they had that he had thrown his entire self into loving her.

Gabrielle's body felt weightless as Cameron made unbridled love to her, making her intimate zones tremble from the heat he filled her with. She screamed out his name as she exploded from sheer ecstasy. She gasped and panted until her breathing became easier.

As he rode the roaring tide of their completion, he'd never felt so amazing.

Completely satisfied and hopelessly in love, Gabrielle looked up at Cameron and smiled. "I hope we always ride those waves of passion together."

Looking at her with love in his eyes, Cameron stroked her hair. "Together is how it will always be for us. I promise."

The couple sealed the pact with a binding kiss.

* * * * *

REQUEST YOUR FREE BOOKS!

2 FREE NOVELS
PLUS 2 *FREE GIFTS!*

KIMANI™
ROMANCE

Love's ultimate destination!

KROM11B

A Brand-New Madaris Family Novel!

NEW YORK TIMES BESTSELLING AUTHOR

BRENDA JACKSON

COURTING JUSTICE

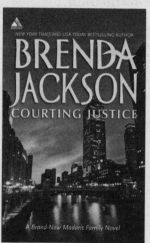

Winning a high-profile case may have helped New York attorney DeAngelo DiMeglio's career, but it hasn't helped him win the woman he loves. Peyton Mahoney doesn't want anything more than a fling with DeAngelo. Until another high-profile case brings them to opposing sides of the courtroom…and then their sizzling attraction can no longer be denied.

"Brenda Jackson is the queen of newly discovered love, especially in her Madaris Family series."
—*BookPage* on *Inseparable*

Available now wherever books are sold.

www.Harlequin.com

KPBJ4730612R